deep in the snow

Alaska Cozy Mystery - 2

wendy meadows

Majestic Owl Publishing LLC
P.O. Box 997
Newport, NH 03773

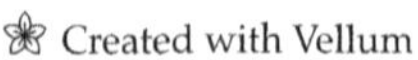

chapter one

Sitting in the small office tucked away in the back of her coffee shop, Sarah watched Amanda dance with a broom like a young high school girl in love. "What in the world are you doing?" Sarah called out.

Amanda continued to dance with the broom, skillfully moving around the kitchen on talented feet as a bitter winter wind cried outside. "I'm remembering my youth," Amanda sang out. "I want to remember what it was like to be young and beautiful before this cold climate shrivels me up into a useless prune."

Sarah leaned back in her chair and continued to watch her friend. "We're not old," she protested even though she felt much older than her mind wanted to admit. Glancing down at the blue wool blend outfit she'd bought in Fairbanks, Sarah wondered if it made her look like an old maid. There was no way she would have even touched the thing in her earlier years. But practicality and awareness of time had somehow crept into her taste in style, destroying hours spent in a closet wondering what to wear and replacing fashionable pieces with simple, warm clothes that were pretty enough to be a little stylish but also tough enough to battle the cold winds of Alaska. "Well, we're not ancient...just...responsible."

Amanda looked at Sarah. "When was the last time you put your hair in a French braid?" she asked.

Sarah lifted her hand and touched her soft hair, which was flowing freely down to the tops of her shoulders. "I cut my hair short after my divorce," she reminded Amanda. "I couldn't do a French braid even if I wanted to."

"You know what I mean." Amanda brought her dance to an end. "Thank you, Mr. Broom, you have been a lovely dancing partner."

Sarah watched as Amanda leaned the broom against the wall next to the back door. Her friend was dressed in a lovely red and white striped candy cane dress that, somehow, seemed to draw out her beauty instead of appearing silly. "Well," Sarah said, glancing at the paperwork sitting on her desk and the green bag resting next to the computer, "we did okay today...nothing great, but we're not in the red."

"We?" Amanda asked, strolling up to the desk. "Los Angeles, this is your coffee shop, not mine. I'm just a poor, lonely beggar that comes along sometimes for a free coffee and cinnamon roll."

Sarah looked up at her friend. "Speaking of cinnamon rolls," she winked, "if you paid me for the ones you've eaten I would be a very wealthy woman."

Amanda stuck her tongue out and smiled. "It's getting a bit late. Maybe we should get ready to leave? My stomach is growling and I'm anxious to cook my shepherd's pie tonight. You're going to love it."

"My poor stomach," Sarah teased. She grabbed the bank bag. "I didn't see Conrad today. He said he might drop by."

"Oh," Amanda grinned. "I see."

"I didn't mean...you know...I mean..." Sarah fumbled. "June Bug, the last thing in the world I'm interested in right now is romance. It's been three days since we've seen Conrad, that's all."

Amanda drew in a deep breath, her nose filling with the

scent of coffee and cinnamon rolls. "Alas, the lost love shall never return," she cried out in a dramatic voice and threw the back of her right hand to her forehead. "Oh, my love, where art thou?"

Sarah leaned against the office doorway and rolled her eyes. "Do you like walking? It's a long way to my cabin."

"Oh, the snow," Amanda cried out again, "why do you torture me so? My love, aren't you supposed to keep me warm? But alas, you are so cold...so cold...so cold..."

Sarah giggled. "Silly."

Amanda smiled and looked at the baking pan still sitting on the stove where a single cinnamon roll greeted her gaze. Sarah followed Amanda's eyes, but before she could say a word, Amanda dashed to the stove and snatched up the cinnamon roll. "We thespians need our energy," she claimed, taking a huge bite of the cinnamon roll and chewing happily. "Your coffee needs work, but your cinnamon rolls...absolutely incredible."

Sarah walked into the kitchen. "Here," she said, picking up a roll of paper towels sitting next to the sink, "you'd better take these along, Mrs. Sticky Fingers."

Amanda held up a pointer finger and motioned for Sarah to hold out the paper towels as she gobbled down the cinnamon roll and quickly washed her hands in the sink. "I don't need the entire roll," she chuckled and tore off enough sheets to dry her hands. "Let's go, Los Angeles."

"Let me get my purse." Sarah walked back to her office. When she picked up the white bag sitting on top of the filing cabinet, the phone on her desk rang. "Even in Alaska someone knows when to call just at the right time," she said to herself. She put down the purse and bank bag. "Hello?"

"Good, you're still at the coffee shop." Conrad's voice seemed calm yet urgent. "Got time to talk?"

"I was just getting ready to drive to the bank and then go home. Amanda is going to make us some of her famous shepherd's pie tonight. Why don't you come over for dinner?" As Sarah spoke, a strong gust of wind struck the back door and kitchen windows. Even though it wasn't snowing and the roads were clear—for the most part—the wind chill was viciously dangerous. "The roads are icy and I really want to get home. I shouldn't have stayed open as long as I did, but a motorcycle group drove through town and stopped in for some coffee."

"The 'Freedom Road Grandpas'," Amanda yelled out from the kitchen, picking up her pink purse from the counter. "A bunch of crazy old men who are going to catch pneumonia. It's a good thing we talked them into staying the night in Fairbanks."

"Yeah, I saw them leave town about a half hour ago," Conrad told Sarah. Sitting in his office, staring out the window, he grew silent and listened to the winds howl outside. "Okay, sure, I'll drive out and have a bite to eat."

"Is anything the matter?" Sarah asked, concerned. "You've been quiet for the last three days. I thought we were friends?"

"We are friends," Conrad assured her. "That's why I'm calling. Sarah, I need your help. I'll explain later. I'll meet you at your place in an hour."

Sarah tried to reply, but Conrad hung up on her. "What's the news?" Amanda asked, walking up to the office door. "What's going on with Mr. New York?"

"I don't know," Sarah answered in a confused voice. "You might want to make extra for dinner tonight because we're going to have a third plate."

Amanda raised her eyebrows. "I see," she smiled.

"Don't start," Sarah groaned. "Come on, let's get going before the roads get worse."

Sarah and Amanda walked out of the kitchen to the wooden coat rack standing next to the front door. "It's going to be absolutely freezing," Amanda said, throwing on her faux fur coat.

"I know." Sarah put on her coat. "Here, hold these."

Amanda held Sarah's purse and the bank bag as Sarah put on her winter gloves and ski cap. "My turn," Amanda said.

Sarah quickly loaded her arms with the two purses and the green bank bag as Amanda covered her hands with warm gloves and put on a thick gray wool hat. As Sarah watched Amanda put on the hat, she smiled. "We're like two peas in a pod, you know that?"

Amanda smiled back. "I know." She looked at the front door. "Ready, Green Bean?"

"Ready, Lima Bean." Drawing in a deep breath, Sarah reached out and pulled open the front door. Crippling, icy winds screamed through the door and attacked them. "Let's move."

"I'm with you!"

As Sarah hurried outside with Amanda, she spotted a black limousine parked across the street. She rushed to lock the front door and dashed away toward her Subaru with Amanda in the lead. The limo sat under a street lamp, casting a long shadow across the snowy street. Inside the limo, a set of dangerous eyes watched Sarah struggle against the winds toward her car.

"In time," a voice spoke from the darkness of the car.

Crawling into the driver's seat, Sarah stared into the rearview mirror at the limo. In her imagination, she saw a hideous, dark creature lurking across the street. "Anyone famous in town?" she asked Amanda.

"You mean that limo?" Amanda asked through chattering teeth. Slamming the passenger's side door shut, she looked at Sarah. "Only me...but I never get a limo."

Sarah buckled her seatbelt. "Buckle up, June Bug," she told Amanda, "we may hit some unexpected ice."

Amanda studied the lowering sun. "Somehow," she said in a worried voice, "when the sun goes down...Snow Falls seems to transform into a scary place. I don't know why. I love this little town, I honestly do. But when the sun sets..."

"I know," Sarah said quietly. "Whenever the sun would set in Los Angeles I'd always feel somber, and a little afraid. The crazies came out at night. When I was a rookie and worked the night shift, tons of bad things happened when the sun went down." Sarah put the Subaru into reverse. "Okay, heat's on. It'll warm up in here soon."

Amanda looked into Sarah's face as her friend backed out into the street. "Why did you become a cop?" she asked curiously. "Some women are happy to stay home, raise a family, bake cookies."

Sarah glanced in the rearview mirror as she eased her car up the street past the sleepy, closed buildings telling the little businesses tucked inside warm bedtime stories. She looked at the limo again. Her cop instincts expected it to follow her, so she was surprised to see it pull out onto the street and take a right onto Candy Pine Avenue.

"I...decided to pursue a career in law enforcement because I wanted to be brave instead of scared," Sarah answered at last. "As a young girl...I was always afraid. I was bullied in high school. I was always so scared to stand up for myself. Then, during my winter break in my senior year of high school, my parents and I took a trip to Colorado."

Amanda leaned back in her seat. "Aspen?"

Sarah shook her head. "No," she sighed. "My dad wanted to go hunting, so we spent a week at a hunting lodge. But," she continued, her voice shifting into a positive tone, "because my dad insisted on staying at the hunting lodge, my life was changed forever."

"I'm all ears."

Sarah carefully came to a stop at a stop sign. Her bank sat up ahead on the left side of the street, nestled in between two brick buildings. "Well," she said as a strong gust of wind rocked the Subaru, "there was a World War II veteran staying at the lodge. His name was Harry Fenney. Mr. Fenney was from Philadelphia and had participated in the Normandy Invasion."

"Many good soldiers died on that beach."

Sarah nodded. "Mr. Fenney was let out on Omaha Beach," she said in a painful voice. "He was eighteen years old when his feet touched the sands of France." She drove through the intersection and the car began crawling up to the bank. Pulling into a parking space, she looked at the single-story wooden building that resembled a small log cabin. "I remember Mr. Fenney telling me how scared he was. He said men were being gunned down right in front of him. And then he asked me if I wanted to see photos of some of his dear friends who had died on the beach."

"Oh my, how sad."

Sarah put the Subaru into neutral. "I saw four photos of young men who didn't look old enough to shave, let alone die in war...their faces still live in my memory today. I remember thinking to myself how brave these men were...and how much of a coward I was. I even told Mr. Fenney those very words. And do you know what he said?"

"What?"

"That sweet and dear old man told me that heroes are those who are afraid but storm the beach anyway," Sarah smiled. "And that's why I became a cop. I decided it was time to storm the beach, live or die. You see, I had to face my fears. I knew becoming a cop would take more courage than I had, but...it was time to storm the beach."

"You did good, Los Angeles." Amanda smiled and patted Sarah on the shoulder. "I wonder what other secrets you have hidden from me?"

"We have a lifetime of friendship to find out each other's secrets," Sarah promised. "Let me drop my deposit into the drop box."

"Hurry," Amanda urged, watching the last bit of daylight vanish behind dark clouds.

Sarah grabbed the green deposit bag and hurried out of the car. Amanda watched her friend slowly make her way up to the right side of the bank, where a metal night deposit drop box sat carved into the outer wall. Sarah quickly made her deposit, glanced up at the dark sky, and then fought the winds and slippery walkway as she struggled back to the Subaru. "All set," she said, climbing into the driver's seat and buckling her seatbelt. "Let's get home."

chapter two

Amanda didn't speak until after they had driven out of town. A bad feeling had settled into her stomach. Why? She didn't know, really. "I'm looking forward to a warm kitchen to cook in," she finally spoke, staring out of the passenger's side window at the shadowy, snow-covered trees swaying back and forth in the powerful winds.

"Who do you suppose was in that limo?" Sarah asked. "I've never seen a limo in town before. Have you or Jack?"

Amanda shook her head. "I thought Jack was going to send a limo to take me out for dinner on our last anniversary, but the jelly roll showed up in his truck. I swear, that man is about as romantic as a porcupine trying to serenade a balloon."

Sarah couldn't help but grin. She loved it when Amanda fussed about her husband's lack of romance. Not that it wasn't serious—but somehow, Amanda made this topic in particular seem harmless and humorous. "Maybe Conrad might know who our special guest is?"

"Just as long as there aren't any more of those creepy snowmen in your writing room when we get to your cabin. Last night I dreamt a snowman wearing a sweater was chasing after me with a cigar in his mouth. I know that's a far cry from a leather-jacket-wearing, candy-cane-chewing, psychotic snowman...but still, I woke up in a blimey cold sweat."

"Without you, June Bug," Sarah said affectionately, "Conrad and I might be dead. We owe you."

"Your friendship is payment enough." Amanda smiled. "I had friends back in London that I was fond of, but never a friend like you. Who would have ever thought a silly American would turn out to be my best friend? What a world we live in."

"Yep, what a world," Sarah agreed. "Hey, turn on the radio and find us a weather report, okay? I think we might be in for some more snow."

Amanda leaned forward, turned on the radio and fished the dial through different stations until she came across a weather report. "Blizzard warning in effect for..." a man with a radio voice began speaking and then faded into static. "In effect for who?" Amanda asked, slapping the radio.

"Winds are disrupting the signal," Sarah said. She leaned forward, looking upward into the dark sky looming over her car. "My gut is telling me we'd better get home, and fast."

"I would say step on it, but I won't," Amanda said and began searching for a different station. "Oh," she pouted and clicked off the radio, "all I'm getting is snow...pardon the pun."

Sarah resisted the urge to press the gas pedal to the floor. Traveling at a slow twenty-five miles per hour down a snowy road that had nothing but snow-covered woods on both sides made her feel as if she was never going to reach home. But finally, after what seemed like hours, she spotted her cabin and smiled. "Home sweet home."

"And we have a guest," Amanda added, pointing at a truck sitting in the driveway.

Sarah pulled into the driveway and eased up next to Conrad's truck as the Subaru's tires crunched under hard, frozen snow. She couldn't see Conrad sitting in the driver's seat, but she did see someone taking a puff from a cigarette or cigar. "I'm glad you're staying with me while Jack is out of town," Sarah told Amanda in a grateful voice.

Amanda looked at Conrad's truck. "You're not afraid of Mr. New York, are you?" she asked, concerned.

"Oh no," Sarah confessed, "I'm just...afraid of what Conrad is going to tell us. It's good to have a friend at your side. I never did like working without a partner in Los Angeles."

"I'm here for you, Los Angeles, bunny slippers and all," Amanda promised. "Now, let's get inside. My shepherd's pie isn't going to cook itself, you know."

"Okay," Sarah said and unbuckled her seatbelt. "Inside we go."

Amanda took her purse, drew in a deep breath, and nodded. "Into the wind we go, first," she said in a voice that sounded like she'd been doused in cold water.

Sarah watched Amanda jump out into the wind. She grabbed her purse and followed. Feeling her boots sink down into ankle-deep snow, she began the tedious task of traveling to the cabin's front door. Conrad opened the driver's side door to his truck and eased out into the wind as well. Sarah was surprised to see the cigar still in his mouth. Stopping at the front of his truck, she looked into Conrad's shadowy face. "Are you coming inside?" she asked over the howling winds.

Conrad nodded. "In a minute," he said. His voice seemed distant.

"No smoking inside," Sarah told him.

"I haven't had a cigar in years," Conrad replied. "I'll explain later."

"I think I already know," Sarah said.

"Hurry up!" Amanda yelled, struggling through the snow.

"Don't be too long," Sarah told Conrad as the winds tore at her beautiful face.

Conrad watched Sarah fight her way to the cabin's front door, unlock it, and hurry inside with Amanda on her tail. Looking down at the cigar in his bare hand, he wondered if allowing Sarah to see the cigar had been such a good idea after all? "Maybe...maybe not," he said. He slung the cigar out into the snow as far as possible and walked to the front door with the bitter winds ripping at his face and hair.

"That man is going to catch his death," Amanda said, running to the fireplace. "He wasn't even wearing a hat to protect his head and ears."

Sarah took off her coat and hung it up on the coat rack next to the front door. "He wasn't even wearing a thick coat."

Before Amanda could respond, Conrad opened the front door and stepped inside. Nodding, he took off his simple black rain jacket and hung it up next to Sarah's coat, revealing a black t-shirt tucked into a pair of blue jeans. "I doubt you dress like that in New York winters," Sarah scolded him. "You're going to catch pneumonia."

Conrad looked down at his black t-shirt. He hadn't even been aware that his outfit wasn't strong enough to protect him from the harsh cold outside. "Yeah, I guess I might need a sweater," he admitted.

"What's going on, Conrad?" Sarah scrunched up her eyebrows.

Conrad looked at Amanda. "Want me to start a fire?"

"Please," Amanda said, still refusing to take off her coat. "I'll go get some coffee going."

Sarah walked over to the couch and sat down. Folding her arms together, she waited to speak until Conrad managed to create a warm and inviting fire in the fireplace.

"You seem like a pro at making fires," she complimented him.

"I grew up in upper New York state," Conrad said as he stood next to the fireplace. "My old man was a serious outdoorsman. He taught me how to track deer when I was really young."

"How does a woodsman like yourself end up as a cop in Brooklyn?"

"Long story," Conrad replied. He warmed his hands. "I guess I do need to remember my gloves next time."

"Seems to me that you have something on your mind," Sarah gently pressed. Settling back on the couch, she watched Conrad warm his hands for a few seconds before speaking again. "I saw a limo in town. Do you know who the limo might belong to?"

"Ralph Gatti," Conrad answered in a direct voice.

Sarah's mouth nearly dropped to the floor. "Ralph Gatti, the mafia crime boss from Boston?"

"That's the guy," Conrad confirmed. "Sarah, you're a cop, so I don't need to go into detail here. I have a week to find out who killed my ex-wife or Gatti is going to kill me. I'm not afraid of the guy. I'm also not stupid enough to believe that I can survive a bare-knuckle fight with him, either."

"What does Ralph Gatti have to do with your ex-wife?" Sarah asked.

"Ralph Gatti was in love with my ex-wife," Conrad explained, keeping his back to her. As he looked into the warm fire, the image of a beautiful Italian woman floated into his mind. "Gatti wanted to marry her, but she didn't care for him. You see, Gatti was at odds with the family her and her brother belonged to. Even though Gatti's headquarters was in Boston, he still had a long reach that extended to New York. Gatti often visited his offices in the five boroughs."

"Offices?"

"Bars, clubs, restaurants, pool halls. He met my ex-wife

when she was working as a cigarette girl in one of his clubs. That was way before we met...she couldn't have been more than nineteen at the time."

"Go on," Sarah said, looking at Conrad's back.

"It was Gatti who brought my ex-wife's..."

"Say her name," Sarah insisted. "Conrad, say your ex-wife's name."

Conrad grew silent and closed his eyes. He listened to the howling winds outside the cabin for a few minutes. "Gatti was the person who brought Sophia's brother into the business. He was a young pup, very impressionable, and easily deceived. He thought becoming a 'Good Fella' would make him something great, when in fact, it made the guy a low life criminal."

"Gatti used Sophia's brother to get to her, then?" Sarah asked in a careful voice.

Conrad nodded. "Yes," he said, opening his eyes. "Sarah, Gatti is in his late sixties now. He had twenty years on Sophia. Sophia...she hung to the arm of Gatti for a while because it was fun, dangerous, and exciting to her. But when Gatti wanted to get serious and slap a ring on her finger, she backed off. He went after Sophia's brother to punish her. But Sophia's brother quickly changed sides and pledged allegiance to the current crime boss in New York, who is running City Hall."

"And that's where you came in," Sarah deducted. "You were assigned to go undercover."

"I went undercover and played a dangerous game with deadly people," Conrad told Sarah. "I honestly thought my cover as a cop would be sniffed out at my first meeting with the crime boss. But I slipped by...don't ask me how, but I did. I was assigned to walk around with Sophia's brother and learn the ropes. I met Sophia a few days later."

Sarah rubbed her chin and stood up. "Gatti's flame for Sophia must have never gone out," she said in a voice that told Conrad she was catching on. "Gatti knows that you went undercover as a cop. He must blame you for Sophia's death."

"And that's why I have one week to find Sophia's killer. Sarah, you and I both know the killer is long gone. A hit was put out on Sophia. I ran into too many dead ends back in New York," Conrad said in frustration. "My last hope was leaving New York and moving here. I thought maybe if I could find a few clues...or even one clue...but so far I'm hitting more dead ends."

"Are you sure Sophia was killed by the mafia?" Sarah asked. "I know that's the logical explanation, but maybe not the correct conclusion. If Gatti is in Snow Falls, he must believe Sophia's killer is here."

"That's a narrow alley you're walking down," Conrad warned. Turning away from the fire, he looked at Sarah. The woman was breathtakingly beautiful. The light from the fire gently glowed across her soft face with delicate kisses. Sarah was so different from Sophia. Sophia had been a wild cat: short-tempered, scrappy, self-centered, daring to the point of stupidity—but Sarah was strong, intelligent, unique, gifted and caring and...clean. Sarah wasn't polluted with the lifestyle of crime that Sophia had been consumed with.

"What are you looking at?" Sarah asked, interrupting Conrad's thoughts.

"I was thinking how much different you are than Sophia. I wish I had been smarter when I met her...but I wasn't. I was stupid. I let looks and fireworks blind me. Sophia was a wild tiger, Sarah. I guess in time we would have ended up divorced anyway...but her death is still my fault. I have to find her killer."

Sarah stared at him. "And what will you do if you find Sophia's killer? Will you make a legal arrest or carry out a personal vendetta?"

Conrad shoved his hands into the front pockets of his jeans. "I will make a legal arrest, even though every fiber of my being wants to make Sophia's killer eat a bullet. I'm a cop, not a vigilante."

Sarah nodded her head. "Good to hear."

Conrad turned back to the fire and looked into the flames. "It is strange that Gatti has traveled from Boston to Alaska. I admit your theory strikes me as plausible. It's possible that Sophia's killer could be in Snow Falls."

"I only suggested that because if Gatti believed Sophia's killer was anywhere else, he would've ordered you to relocate to wherever he believes the killer is," Sarah explained.

"You're a smart woman who knows her stuff," Conrad said warmly.

"So, do you agree with my theory?"

"Gatti is staying close," Conrad answered simply, ignoring her question.

"Coffee," Amanda announced, walking into the living room carrying three brown mugs of coffee on a wooden serving tray. She paused, looking at Sarah and then at Conrad. "Blimey, you could cut the tension in this room with a butcher's knife."

Conrad turned and focused on Amanda. "I need your help," he told her sternly. "Sarah trusts you, so I'm gonna trust you. I need you to team up and be her partner. Together, the three of us have one week to save my life and find a killer. Are you game?"

Amanda didn't know what to say or how to reply. She looked at Sarah for understanding and help. "She's game," Sarah answered for her, and picked up a mug from the serving tray. "We have one week. Let's get busy."

chapter three

After dinner, Conrad excused himself and went outside to his truck. He returned to the kitchen carrying a black briefcase. Taking a minute to defrost, he sat down at the kitchen table and sipped on a hot cup of coffee. "The contents of the briefcase hold all I have about Sophia's murder," he explained.

Sarah walked to the kitchen table and sat down next to Amanda. Stuffed from two plates of delicious shepherd's pie and a slice of homemade apple pie, she felt ready to burst. "I can't believe I polished off two whole plates," she told Amanda.

Amanda smiled and sipped on a mug of coffee. "We British know a thing or two about the kitchen."

Conrad agreed. "Dinner was delicious. I haven't eaten so much in one sitting in years."

"Thank you," Amanda said. "Now if only I could get my husband to eat shepherd's pie. That bloke refuses to even look at it. Why? Who knows? I married a strange one."

Conrad put down his coffee mug. "Okay," he said, focusing on the briefcase, "let's get started."

Sarah patiently watched Conrad open the briefcase and pull out three brown folders. He handed Sarah and Amanda a folder each and kept one for himself. "Each folder contains the same information. Unfortunately, there isn't much information to dissect."

Sarah opened the folder in her hand and began exploring the contents: photos of members of two different crime families, arrest reports, copies of passports, credit card receipts, addresses, court dates, license plate numbers, tax records, car rental papers. "Conrad, there is a great deal of information to decipher here," she said, shuffling through the papers.

"All dead ends," Conrad said in a miserable voice. "I've checked out every member of each crime family. I checked passports, arrest reports, credit card purchases, car rentals...nothing. All the faces you see before you were in New England when Sophia was killed...every last stinking one of them has a credible alibi."

"The Gatti Family and the Riva Family are well-established organized crime families," Sarah explained to Amanda. "The Gatti Family works mainly out of Boston, but still has areas in New York under their control. The Riva Family hasn't been around too long...twenty years at the most, I'd say. The Riva family went to war with the Sarti Family and came out the victor. Most of the Sarti Family integrated into the Riva Family when the war was over. This caused the Gatti Family to become weaker in New York because the Riva Family now had parts of the Sarti Family under their control."

Conrad listened to Sarah explain the two crime families to Amanda with admiration and curiosity. "You seem to know a lot about the mafia," he pointed out.

Sarah kept shifting through the papers in the folder. "Los Angeles is polluted with the Trapini Family," she replied. "The Trapini Family is well known for running drugs for the Gatti Family while running guns for the Sarti Family. I found more than one body washed up on the beach or stuffed into a dumpster in some ugly alley as a result of bad blood between them."

Amanda wasn't sure what she was looking at or what to even be looking for. Frustrated, she closed the folder in her hands and placed it down on the kitchen table. "Mr. New York," she said, "where is the report from our police department?"

Conrad reached into his briefcase and pulled out a fourth folder. "This report is not to leave this kitchen," he warned Sarah and Amanda. "It's been classified by the FBI. The Feds get touchy when someone dies under their protection. Not that Sophia wanted their protection to begin with. What choice did she have, though?"

"Stop punishing yourself," Sarah told him gently. "Conrad, Sophia is dead and there is nothing you or anyone can do to bring her back. What matters now is finding her killer and saving your life."

"Do you really think Gatti is going to let me live even if I do find Sophia's killer?" Conrad asked. He sounded exhausted. "Let's face it, Gatti is going to feed me a bullet whether I find the person who killed my ex-wife or not."

Sarah didn't reply. She knew Conrad was probably right. "Here," Amanda said, taking the folder from Conrad, "let me have a look. I'm not a cop, but my cousin worked for Scotland Yard before he crippled his leg in a hiking accident. He used to tell me about his work all the time. Maybe some of his wits will help me?"

Conrad bit his lower lip and looked at the folder in his hand. "My career is on the line here...and so is my life," he reminded her, and reluctantly relinquished the folder as a powerful gust of icy wind began shaking the cabin.

Sarah scooted her chair closer to Amanda and studied the report with her friend. "Okay, let's see what we have here."

Conrad watched Sarah and Amanda study the report together. Picking up his coffee mug, he sipped on the hot brew and waited. Although he knew the report by heart, he hoped that Sarah and Amanda might catch something—a minor detail, no matter how small—that he might have missed. "Well?" he finally asked.

"Your ex-wife was found with money in her purse," Amanda said, confused. "She was found fully clothed, wearing a warm winter coat, yet the cause of her death was ruled as hypothermia."

"Sophia's body was found off to the side of a well-traveled ski trail north of town, next to a boulder," Sarah continued, reading from the page in front of her. "The coroner states that she had been dead at least three days before her body was discovered by a Park Ranger patrolling the area. If I'm not mistaken, Conrad, that time frame puts us—"

"The snowstorm!" Amanda interrupted. "Oh, sorry for interrupting, love."

"Don't be sorry," Sarah said. "That's what I was going to say. We make a good team."

Amanda smiled proudly. "Yes, we do."

"Snowstorm?" Conrad asked, confused. Setting down the coffee mug, he leaned over the table and snatched the folder from Amanda's hands. "The report states that the weather was clear," he said, reviewing the report. "Why would Sophia have ventured out into a snowstorm...and why would the Feds lie about the weather report?"

"Here's another question," Sarah said. "Why would a hitman follow Sophia into a snowstorm? Conrad, we both know how the mafia operates. No hitman hired by the mafia is going to drag a person out into a snowstorm and wait until they freeze to death."

Conrad slammed the folder down onto the table and jumped to his feet. "Are you ladies sure about the snowstorm?" he asked. "I mean, are you absolutely sure?"

"Mr. New York," Amanda said in a stern tone, "I may not be a bloody genius, but I know how to check the weather reports each morning. On the night the snowstorm tipped a wink, I was in my kitchen with my husband Jack baking muffins. Afterward, we played a game of Scrabble and cuddled in front of the fireplace together. I remember because it's not often my husband and I have nights like that because we're arguing over our son most of the time."

"I was in my writing room when the snowstorm arrived," Sarah told Conrad. "I remember how powerful the winds were and that I was worried that the power might go off. Somehow the power remained on, though."

Conrad wasn't sure what to make of the new information. "That means Sophia might have attempted to escape? But why? She didn't have any Feds watching her. The Feds stuck Sophia up here and told her to be a good girl if she wanted to live. Sophia didn't mind throwing curveballs at me, but she was terrified of the Sarti Family. She hated the Feds but knew if she wanted to stay alive, she needed to accept being hidden in the Witness Protection Program."

"Did Sophia ever give up any information on the Sarti Family?" Sarah asked.

Conrad shook his head no. "The Feds put her on ice up here, hoping that she would come around and spill what she had on the Sarti Family."

"Maybe the poor woman knew someone was out to kill her and tried to escape in the snowstorm?" Amanda asked.

"The snowstorm," Sarah whispered and stood up. She walked to the coffee pot sitting on the kitchen counter and studied the coffee inside. "I'll make a fresh pot," she said.

"Wait," Conrad ordered, "tell me what you're thinking first. I can read your face, Sarah. This is not the time to hold back on me."

Sarah leaned back against the kitchen counter. "The police report doesn't give the location of Sophia's residence here in Snow Falls. What was her address?"

Amanda looked at Conrad. Conrad rubbed his eyes. "184

Snow Bird Lane," he said. "The address belongs to a little one-bedroom cabin north of town. I checked out the cabin, though. It's clean. All of Sophia's personal belongings were removed."

Sarah struggled to connect the dots. "We need to speak to Andrew."

"I already have," Conrad informed her. "It worked this way. The park ranger who found my ex-wife's body called the police. Chief Cunningham went out to the trail with Officer Andrew and Officer Edwin. He didn't even know Sophia was under the Feds' protection. It wasn't until later, when Sophia's death was put across the wire, that the Feds jumped into action and sent a man from Anchorage to talk with Chief Cunningham."

"And from there, the official report was altered?" Sarah asked Conrad, fishing for his opinion.

Conrad shook his head. "Andrew told me that Sophia was fully clothed when they found her. Her purse was lying next to her body, untouched. He told me it was clear that my ex-wife had frozen to death. She was wearing a thick coat, but nothing strong enough to protect her from the winds and freezing temperatures for a long period of time, especially during the night."

"Why would she head north and not south?" Sarah asked. "Why would your ex-wife run on foot and not in a vehicle? You said no federal agent was watching her."

"I've asked myself that question many times," Conrad confessed and ran his hands through his hair. "Sophia could have easily ditched town and vanished. She was given a Subaru, much like the one you drive, to get around town."

Amanda, who had been carefully listening to the exchange, finally spoke. "She ran scared," she said. "That's the only explanation that makes sense. New York, your ex-wife got spooked and ran scared into the night, hoping to hide in the snowstorm."

"I agree," Sarah said in a confident tone. "You said her body was found next to a boulder, right?"

"Andrew said the way Sophia's body was found...well, it looked like she was trying to use the boulder as some form of shelter against the storm," Conrad explained. "But I'm not naive, either. I've worked homicide for many years, too, Sarah. Sophia could've just as easily been murdered, and then the murderer made it appear that she'd frozen to death."

"The mafia always kills viciously, so why would they frame it as an accidental death?" Sarah pointed out.

"Maybe the person sent to kill Sophia was ordered to make her talk before she died?" Conrad snapped. "Hey, I'm sorry," he immediately apologized. "There was no excuse for that."

"You're under a lot of pressure," Sarah said gently. "I've snapped at my own people many times, too."

Amanda saw fatigue eating at Conrad's eyes. "New York," she said calmly, "you did say the cabin your ex-wife was living in was found untouched?"

Conrad nodded. "No signs of a forced entry...even the blasted toilet was squeaky clean."

"Steve Mintfield," Amanda said, turning in her chair to face Sarah.

"Who?" Sarah asked.

"Steve Mintfield," Amanda said again. "Steve is retired and builds cabinets in a workshop on his property. He's also a locksmith."

"Ah," Sarah said and looked at Conrad.

"The cabin is owned by a rental company in Fairbanks. I'll see who makes their keys for them," Conrad said quickly.

"Could be an imposter showed up at Mr. Mintfield's place, pretending to be from the rental company, and requested additional keys be made?" Sarah suggested. "Conrad, that's a solid lead."

Conrad nodded his head and sat down at the kitchen

table. "I knew asking you ladies for help wasn't a bad idea," he said, stifling a yawn.

"It's late," Sarah rose to her feet. "I think we need to call it a night."

Conrad checked the watch on his wrist. "It's almost midnight. I'd better get going. I'll meet you both in town at your coffee shop tomorrow around noon. Sound good?"

Sarah didn't answer, listening to the winds howl and cry outside. Amanda read her worried face. "New York," Amanda said, standing up, "you're sleeping on the couch tonight. You're not properly dressed to go out in this weather."

"I agree," Sarah said in relief. "You'll freeze before the cab of your truck warms up. You're staying here tonight. No arguments."

Conrad yawned again. The idea of fighting the winds outside didn't exactly appeal to him. "My truck does take some time to warm up," he admitted, "but I don't want to impose."

"You're not imposing," Sarah promised. "Now, let's all get ready for bed. I have a feeling we're going to have a very long day tomorrow."

"I've still got insomnia," Conrad told Sarah. "I'll be lucky to get four hours."

"Try," Sarah urged him. "Lie down, close your eyes, and try to relax your mind. I know I'm asking the impossible, but unless you get some rest you won't be any good to yourself or us. Please."

Conrad looked down at his mug of coffee. "Sure," he said, caving in. "And thanks."

Amanda walked over to him, patted his shoulder, and walked away toward the spare bedroom. "Don't let the couch bugs bite," she called out over her shoulder.

"I'll go get you some covers," Sarah told Conrad and left the kitchen.

Left alone, Conrad picked up the folder holding the police report as anger flushed into his cheeks. Narrowing his eyes, he whispered, "I think we might have a dirty Fed on our hands."

Outside in the dark night, the winds continued to howl as a steady stream of snow began to fall.

chapter four

Ralph Gatti walked into Sarah's coffee shop with two men following closely behind him. Without saying a word, he sat down at a table close to the back wall, removed his thick black overcoat, handed the coat to one of his men, and folded his arms together. "He's tough-looking," Amanda whispered, staring at Gatti from the kitchen door.

Sarah examined the vicious, deadly face marked with scars and anger. "He's a tough customer," Sarah whispered back.

"And bald," Amanda murmured, looking at the gray fedora resting on Gatti's head. "One of us should go out there."

"Steve Mintfield is due here any minute," Sarah said in a worried voice. "And Conrad is at the police station. I don't like the idea of taking on Gatti alone – not if he knows that Conrad's asked for my help."

"Service," Gatti boomed impatiently as his two men stepped behind him and folded their arms together.

Sarah drew in a deep breath. "You stay here in the kitchen. If any shooting starts, make a dash for the back door."

Amanda grabbed Sarah's hand. "I'm...coming with you," she said nervously.

Sarah pulled her hand away and looked into Amanda's eyes. "Please," she begged, "stay in the kitchen. There's no sense in both of us possibly risking our lives. You have Jack and your son to think about."

"I..." Amanda began to speak and then slowly nodded her head. "Okay, Los Angeles. I'll stay in the kitchen."

Sarah patted her friend's shoulder and walked out into the main room. "What will it be?" she asked in a friendly tone.

Gatti gave Sarah a hard look. He had expected a tough Los Angeles street cop, but instead saw a pretty woman dressed in a thick green sweater falling over a gray wool dress. "Coffee," he sounded angry.

Sarah shifted her eyes away from Gatti and glanced at the two statue-like men standing behind him. Both of Gatti's men were wearing black overcoats and gray fedoras. They looked like twins, even though it was clear that one man was in his twenties and the other man was in his forties. "Sure," Sarah said and called out "Three coffees!" toward the kitchen.

Gatti didn't take his eyes off Sarah. "Sarah Garland," he huffed, unamused. "I expected more from a woman with your reputation."

"Oh?" Sarah kept her voice calm. "Do you know me?"

Gatti frowned. "Knock off the act," he warned her, keeping his arms folded. "You know who's sitting in front of you. So, if you decide you want to play games with me, just remember the games you play can quickly become very painful."

"Don't you threaten me," Sarah snapped. "Sure, I know who you are, and I couldn't care less."

The bodyguard in his twenties reached for his gun. Gatti shook his head. "Leave her be," he growled. Keeping his eyes locked on Sarah, he took a minute to study her face. "I assume Detective Spencer has spoken to you by now?"

"Yes," Sarah said, maintaining eye contact with Gatti.

"Sit down."

"I'll stand."

"Sit...down...now," Gatti ordered through gritted teeth.

"I'll stand," Sarah repeated angrily.

Gatti nodded. The man in his forties walked over to Sarah, grabbed her arm, and forced her to sit down. Sarah didn't resist. Knowing that resisting would surely lead to pain, she decided to play along. "Sophia," Gatti said as his bodyguard moved back behind him, "was murdered. I have given Detective Spencer seven days to locate the person who murdered her."

"Why do you care?" Sarah asked, rubbing her right arm.

Gatti unfolded his arms and slowly rubbed the long scar running across his forehead. "Help Detective Spencer find the garbage that murdered Sophia and I will let you live, as well as your friend standing behind the kitchen door. The seven-day rule now applies to the both of you as well as Detective Spencer. I want no games."

"Will you really let Detective Spencer live?" Sarah asked defiantly. "Come on, pal, we both know you hate cops. And it was Detective Spencer who married the woman you loved, a woman who refused to become your wife."

Gatti balled his right hand into a fist and struck the table. "One more word and you're a dead woman!" he yelled.

"So kill me already," Sarah said. "Listen, Gatti, you can go around bullying people as much as you want, but up here in Alaska, you're walking on thin ice. I have friends in this town who can pick an antler off a moose at five hundred feet. Up here, there aren't any rules. You can kill me, but if you do, trust me, you'd better get out of town and fast."

"Mr. Gatti ain't afraid of anyone," the man in his twenties informed Sarah.

"And a bullet fired from a hunting rifle doesn't ask names," Sarah fired back. "You're aware of the weather outside. A storm is moving in. The roads leading in and out of town will be inaccessible come nightfall. So you'd better knock off the threats or else carry them out and get out of town."

Gatti stared at Sarah. He was aware that Snow Falls was unfriendly territory. "Find Sophia's killer. You have seven days."

"And then what?" Sarah asked. "What if we can't find Sophia's killer? Are you really going to kill us? And for what? No, Gatti, you have no intention of killing anyone, so knock off the threats. It's clear you loved Sophia, and I can understand your anger. My friend and I are going to work with Detective Spencer and look under every stone there is. But you have to realize that the person who killed Sophia may not be in Snow Falls."

"He's here," Gatti assured her. "And let me tell you something, cop. In seven days, if I don't have the skunk who murdered Sophia gift wrapped and delivered to me, you will die. I can make one phone call and have an army of men here within the next twenty-four hours. If you want a war, I'll give you a war. But the deaths of innocent people will be on your conscience. Don't try and play rough with me, because I hit hard and without mercy."

Gatti's eyes told Sarah that he was clearly speaking the truth. She and Amanda now had seven days to live unless the murderer was located. "You said 'he.' Why?" Sarah asked, deciding to drop into her investigative mode. "How do you know the person who killed Sophia is a male? And how do you know that person is still in Snow Falls? And," she added, narrowing her eyes, "if you believe the person who killed Sophia is in Snow Falls, why aren't you going after him yourself?"

Gatti didn't like being questioned by a cop. He decided to toss out a few bread crumbs and nothing more. "I don't have facts," he told her in a low, dangerous voice. "What I do know is that my search has ended here. And that's all you need to know. You have seven days."

"Why seven days?" Sarah insisted. "If you want to catch the killer, why not offer more time?"

"Seven days," Gatti roared and hit the table again. "I'm an impatient man. Don't test me, cop."

"Get out of my coffee shop," Sarah pointed at the front door, "and don't come back in here until the seven days are over. By then, we'll have your killer sitting right where you're sitting now."

Gatti stood up. "If you fail me," he warned, "your kitchen will be decorated with funeral wreaths."

"Get out."

Gatti narrowed his eyes and looked at Sarah. "Seven days," he promised. "And cancel the coffee."

Sarah watched Gatti put his coat back on and walk outside.

"Are you crazy?" Amanda asked, bursting through the kitchen door the instant he was gone. "Of course, you are," she answered herself, and hurried to check Sarah's arm. "That brute grabbed you awful hard."

"I'm okay," Sarah promised. She stood up, looked at the front door and shook her head. "Gatti knows who the killer is. He has to. Something isn't right, Amanda. I have a bad feeling about this one."

Before Amanda could answer, a man in his late sixties walked through the front door, covered with snow. "Snow's starting to really come down," Steve Mintfield said through chattering teeth. Stomping snow off his brown boots onto the red and green floor mat, he looked around. "I didn't think anyone would be crazy enough to come into town today except me."

Sarah watched Steve take off his thick brown coat and hang it up on the wooden coat rack. "Coffee?" she asked.

"Please," Steve said, pulling off a pair of gray gloves and sticking them into his back pocket.

Amanda gave Sarah a worried look and hurried back to the kitchen. "Please, sit down," Sarah told Steve, pointing at the chair Gatti had been sitting in.

Steve smiled and complied. "So," he said, looking around at the warm and comfortable room, "where is this new detective I've heard so much about?"

"Actually…" Sarah paused, preparing for a tongue lashing. "Detective Spencer is at the police station. He's asked me to take his place."

Instead of becoming upset, Steve nodded his head. "I've only seen you a handful of times," he told Sarah, "but the way folks around town talk about you, well, it's impressive. Years back I traveled to Los Angeles to attend my daughter's wedding, and let me say, that was enough for me. I can't imagine working as a homicide detective in that city. I'm just grateful my daughter moved away to Tennessee."

Sarah sat down. "Mr. Mintfield," she said, struggling to place her thoughts in order, "I sure do appreciate you coming out on such an awful day."

"Ain't nothing," Steven said in a warm voice. "I've always liked the snow. The snow and me, we're old friends."

Amanda rushed out of the kitchen with a white mug full of hot coffee. "Very hot," she told Steve, setting the coffee down in front of him. "Cream...sugar?"

"Nope, coffee was meant to be guzzled down black. Now, why don't you ladies stop being so nervous and talk to me? I don't bite, you know."

"Mr. Mintfield—"

"Steve," he corrected, taking a sip of his coffee. "Ah, nice and strong, just the way I like it. Some folks say you make your coffee too strong, but me, well, the stronger the better."

Sarah felt a smile touch her lips. Steve Mintfield was a

warm and charming man. "Steve, did you pass three men outside?"

"Strange looking fellas," Steve said. "Never saw them before in my life. Did they give you any trouble?"

"No...not exactly," Amanda answered before Sarah could speak.

"Steven, can you keep a secret? What I mean to ask you is...can we trust you?" Sarah asked.

Steve put down his coffee and looked at Sarah. His face became serious. "Now, I make it clear that I keep to my own business," he said. "I don't get mixed up in other people's problems. My wife and I are peaceful people. We keep to ourselves, treat others as we want to be treated, and more than anything we fear God. Is that clear?"

"Yes, sir," Sarah said, expecting him to stand up, walk out of her coffee shop and never look back.

"But," he continued, looking around the empty room and then up at Amanda, "if this is about that woman's death, then...well, I guess I can make an exception."

Amanda put her hand down on Sarah's shoulder. "You know about—"

Steve held up his right hand. "I know a woman was found dead. Now," he said calmly, "I'm not very happy about a murder taking place in our town, especially a murder Chief Cunningham is keeping under his hat. I only found out because some suit came out to my land and hired me to go out to the dead woman's cabin and put new locks on her doors. I also had to replace the back door altogether. It had been kicked off the hinges."

Sarah looked up at Amanda. "What did you see while you were replacing the locks and the back door? Was anything in the cabin?"

"I kept my eyes low and worked with my mouth shut," he replied. "Three suits were clearing the cabin faster than I could work."

"Steve," Sarah persisted patiently, "before this federal agent showed up on your land, did anyone else show up there?"

Steven rubbed his chin. "I make cabinets. The rental company that owns the cabin the dead woman lived in hired me to make a set of kitchen cabinets and to put new locks on the doors. But...oh...a week or so before the suit showed up on my land, a strange fellow came around asking for a set of keys to the cabin in question. He said he was from the rental company, but I knew better. I've met the man from the rental company. The fellow got mighty angry with me when I refused to give him a set of keys. I ended up having to put my hunting rifle in his face and run him off."

"What did this man look like? Can you describe him?"

"Big fellow. He was wearing a gray coat and brown pants with fancy shoes. His hair was bushy and red. Neatly trimmed beard. He was wearing glasses, too. And I remember how neatly trimmed his fingernails were. To be honest, I guess the fellow could have been from the rental company from the way he looked, but I knew better."

"Did you make a report?" Amanda asked.

"Nah. What would bothering the chief have accomplished? All he could have done was send someone out to take a statement from me. The fellow requesting the keys could have easily denied any claims I made against him. It was better to just let the matter drop."

Sarah rested her chin in her hands and peered across the table into Steve's face. "You said the back door to the rental cabin had been kicked open?"

"Yep," Steve said, "and the wooden floor inside the kitchen door was damaged. It was clear a good deal of snow had piled up on the floor. I even found large wet spots on the living room carpet."

"Indicating that the snow from outside had been blowing into the cabin for quite some time," Sarah concluded.

Steve agreed. "That back door must've been off the hinges for at least a full day, if not more." Looking down at his coffee, Steve grew quiet for a minute. "The man who I ran off my land killed the woman, didn't he? I've run my brain around this problem a few times and...well, I know I can't exactly blame myself for the woman's death, but I guess I should have called the chief and made a statement."

"You did what you thought was right," Sarah assured him.

"I agree," Amanda added. "And honestly, what would Andy and Barney have done? Let's face it, we don't have a squad of Einsteins on our local police force."

"Maybe not, but each man in uniform is a good man," Steve answered. He looked up at Sarah. "Sure was strange how those suits were running around so fast at that cabin. They cleared the place before I could finish putting on the last lock. And my paycheck came from the FBI, not the rental company, too. Is that helpful?"

"Could be," Sarah replied in a grateful tone. Her gaze rested on Steve's mug, and she suddenly hungered for a cup of coffee herself. "Did you see what was carried out of the cabin?"

"Mostly cardboard boxes," he explained. "There was a large white moving truck parked outside. The three FBI guys got all the furnishings out into the truck first and then packed up the small stuff. I heard them fussing to themselves a few times...snapping at each other as they worked."

"Did you hear why they were being fussy with each other?" Amanda asked.

"I'm not an eavesdropper," Steve said, sounding proud of himself, "but...sure, I heard. How could I not have heard?"

Sarah tensed up in her chair. "Is it okay to ask what you heard?" she asked carefully.

Steve picked up his mug and took a sip of coffee. "A book," he said simply. "Those three suits kept fussing over a book. I kept hearing them say 'The book has to be in the cabin somewhere.'"

"Book?" Sarah whispered to herself. She paused, unsure what to ask next. "Amanda—"

But Amanda had already read Sarah's mind. "You want coffee. I'm on it. I could use a cup myself. Steve, would you like a hot cinnamon roll?"

Steve patted his stomach. "Oh no, thank you. Lana has me on a strict diet. If I cheat with a cinnamon roll, Lana will shove my head into her oven."

Amanda smiled at him. Sure, Steve wasn't a British man with a dignified tongue, she thought; he was just a simple, kind, hard-working American who appreciated the simple things in life and believed in being honest. "I'll be back in a jiff," she said.

"Steve, did you leave the cabin before or after the FBI agents?" Sarah asked.

"Those three suits left me alone. After they packed up, one of them told me that my check would be in the mail, asked me for the key to the new locks, and left. That's it."

"Did it seem like they'd found the book in question?"

Steve shook his head no. "No way. They were extremely grumpy when they finally left. I have to admit, I took longer than needed on the door and locks. I guess I did that because I kinda liked to see the suits unhappy."

"Did you walk around the cabin before you left?"

"I sure did," Steve said, lowering his voice secretively. "I know the builder who put the cabin up. He's not an honest man...cuts corners, buys cheap material, bribes the building inspector...those kinds of things." Steve took a sip of coffee. "You see, when I installed the cabinets I built, I had the chance to inspect the quality of the cabin, but...well, something about the place somehow seemed different, and I didn't know what."

"Oh?" Sarah prompted.

"The quality of the cabin is, well...junk. I could barely get the cabinets I built to stay up on the walls. I'm not saying the quality changed...only..." Steve scratched the back of his head. "*Something* was changed."

"Could you find out what?" Sarah gently pressed.

Steve took another sip. "Nah," he said. "I built the cabinets over four years ago. I don't have the best memory, either. All I know is that something seemed different from the last time I was in the cabin. I'm kinda anal that way...when something doesn't sit right with me, I have to take a look around and investigate."

Sarah sat silently for a couple of minutes, assembling the information Steve had revealed to her into a neat file in her mind. "Have you ever seen the red-headed man since? Maybe around town?" she asked, expecting a flat 'No' as an answer.

But Steve surprised her. "Yeah," he answered. "I saw the guy at Jacob's grocery store a couple of days before that snowstorm hit us last month. Speaking of which, I'm worried the storm brewing outside now is going to be a tad worse."

Sarah drew in a deep breath. "Was he with a woman?"

Steve shook his head. "No, that fellow was parked out front in a red truck. I don't think he even recognized me. But, you know what, now that you mention it...maybe he *was* with someone?"

"Or maybe he was watching someone," Sarah added. "When you left the grocery store, was the red truck still parked outside?"

Steve shook his head again and finished off his coffee. "No," he said. He began to stand up. "But you know," he said, pausing halfway up, "when I walked into the grocery store, a woman I had never seen before was fussing with a cashier... I mean, this woman was really raising the roof. She had a funny accent, too. Lana and me, we didn't pay her much mind, though. We figured she was an out-of-towner and went on with our shopping."

"What did this woman look like?"

Steve thought back to the day that he and his wife of thirty-five years had walked into Jacob's grocery store. "It was mighty cold, and Lana was in a rush to get inside. The store was crammed full of folks, like sardines in a can. I just kinda glanced over at the fussing woman...all I really remember about her was that she was awful pretty to have such an ugly attitude."

Sarah nodded. "What color hair did she have?"

Steve struggled to remember but finally tossed out blonde as the hair color.

"Steve, you have been wonderful. I can't thank you enough."

"Maybe you can drive some customers my way, then," Steve sighed. "Business is tight."

"Sure," Sarah smiled. "The cabinets in my kitchen are old and I've been planning to replace them, along with the bathroom cabinet. I also wanted a bookshelf built for my living room, if you're interested?"

"You bet I'm interested," Steve beamed.

"Great," Sarah smiled again. "Please, wait right here." She rushed into the kitchen, noticed Amanda sitting in her office talking on the phone, grabbed her purse, and ran back out to Steve. Opening her purse, she pulled out a checkbook. "This is only a deposit," she said, writing out a check. "I'll cover the difference when you come up with an exact quote."

Steve took the check from Sarah. His eyes went wide. "That's some deposit. I can't accept this."

"Take it," Sarah insisted. "Please."

Steve looked at her warmly. "I'll make sure to do really good work on your cabinets," he promised. "I'd better be getting home now."

"I'll call you in eight days," Sarah promised and walked Steve to the door. After he left, Sarah ran back to her office just as Amanda was ending her call. "Who was that?"

"That was Mr. New York. He has some news for us and wants us to come to the police station right away."

"Let's close down and get moving," Sarah said in an urgent tone. Just then, she heard the front door of the shop open and she sighed. "The last thing I need right now is a customer."

She walked into the front room and stopped in her tracks. A man with bushy red hair was sitting down at a table. The man looked at Sarah, and she saw a mysterious look in his eyes. "I'll have a coffee," he said with a confident voice.

"One coffee," Sarah yelled through the kitchen door at Amanda. "We have cinnamon rolls too if you'd like."

"Just coffee," the man said. He hadn't taken off the dark green coat he was wearing. "I saw Steve Mintfield leave," he added abruptly. "On a day like today, a man like Steve Mintfield doesn't travel into town just for a cup of coffee."

"He might," Sarah said. She was still standing behind the front counter, keeping a safe distance from the man. "Do you know Steve?"

"Not personally."

Amanda pried the kitchen door open and handed Sarah a mug full of coffee. Sarah took the coffee and placed it down on the counter. "Here's your coffee. If you need anything, I'll be in the kitchen."

"Ralph Gatti is in town," the man said as he stood up. He walked over to the front counter, picked up the mug of coffee and took a sip. "I noticed that he paid you a visit today as well, Detective Sarah Garland."

"Who are you?" Sarah demanded.

"Someone with answers," the man said, locking eyes with her. "If you help me, I'll help you."

"Help you?"

"Gatti wants the same thing I want. He's not here playing Romeo. He stopped loving Sophia many years ago. Sophia had to protect her brother, though, didn't she? Of course she did."

Intuition and facts rallied together in Sarah's mind, and she let her accusation fly out of her mouth. "You killed Sophia, didn't you?" She braced for his response.

But the man merely shook his head and continued to stare at her with icy eyes. "If you want answers, help me. If you refuse, then so be it. But let me warn you: Gatti will carry out his threat against you, Detective Garland. I know you have seven days to find the killer. I can help you."

"Who are you?" Sarah demanded again.

"I'll be in touch." The man took another sip of coffee. "A bit too strong," he commented, and then he was gone.

Sarah drew in a deep breath, resisting the urge to call out to him and demand more answers. Instead, she quietly watched him leave her coffee shop and walk outside into the snowstorm. "Well," Amanda said, walking out of the kitchen, "this has been a very interesting morning, to say the least."

chapter five

"The day seems to be just beginning," Sarah said to Amanda as she looked around the front room. "Maybe I should turn this place into a fancy tea room, add some pretty furnishings, put some expensive paintings up on the walls, purchase a lovely carpet...maybe then I won't feel like my coffee shop is a beacon for criminals."

"You would be flat broke in a week," Amanda teased. "Come on, let's go see what New York has to say. Oh, and he wants a to-go coffee, please, ma'am, and a cinnamon roll."

"At least someone likes my coffee," Sarah sighed. She looked at the front door. Outside, danger was dancing in the snowstorm with a heart of ice.

Conrad munched on his cinnamon roll hungrily. "Haven't had a chance to eat yet," he said.

"You were gone when we woke up this morning." Sarah was standing by the window in his office, feeling slightly amused as she watched Conrad devour the roll.

Amanda took off her coat and put it down on the chair

sitting in front of Conrad's desk, and then briskly brushed a few pieces of lint off the pink sweater she was wearing over her warm yellow dress. "So what's the news, New York? You sounded urgent on the phone."

Conrad polished off the cinnamon roll and grabbed a brown paper cup full of coffee that was now lukewarm instead of hot. Still dressed in his black t-shirt and blue jeans from last night, he looked rough and exhausted. "I made a few calls this morning. My first call was to McLeary's Cabin Rentals in Fairbanks. I got the exact date that Sophia moved into the cabin. The date does not match the date on her records that a friend in Washington dug up for me earlier this morning. There is exactly a two-week discrepancy between the date on Sophia's file and the date on file at McLeary's." Conrad chugged some coffee down.

"What does that mean?" Amanda asked, confused.

"It means that Sophia had a two-week vacation before she arrived in Alaska."

Sarah looked through the Venetian blinds covering the window. Out on the snow-covered front street, a black limo crawled past the police station. "Gatti paid me a visit," she told Conrad. "It now seems that Amanda and I have seven days to live, too, unless we help you locate the man who killed Sophia. Gatti is certain the killer is a man and that the killer is still in Snow Falls."

"Club buddy." Amanda's attempt to joke with Conrad failed because Conrad, lost in thought, hadn't even heard her. Plopping down in the chair across from Conrad, she sighed miserably. "You know, Jack is going to take me back to London after all of this. Not that I would mind; I miss London. But I do love my new home, too." Amanda looked at Conrad, then at Sarah. She realized she was talking to herself, as the two of them were completely wrapped up in the case.

Conrad leaned back in his office chair. "What else did Gatti say?"

"That's about it," Sarah replied. "He just rode past the police station in his limo, though. I think he's making laps around the block."

"The way the snow is falling, he won't be making laps too much longer," Conrad said. "The man who operates the plow that runs through town hurt his ankle this morning. He's having his brother take over the plowing, but his brother won't be able to start for another hour or so."

"By then the roads might be impassable," Amanda pointed out.

"If we could find out where Gatti is staying, maybe we can trap him?" Sarah suggested. "Of course, that would be foolish," she added hastily.

Conrad frowned. "Gatti is staying at the hotel in town. It would be wise to leave the hornet's nest alone for now."

"You bet we will," Amanda promised. "I've seen some mean blokes in my time, but that guy puts the cherry on the ice cream."

"Cake," Sarah corrected.

"Poison cake," Amanda shivered.

"Conrad, we also spoke to Steve Mintfield," Sarah said, turning away from the window. She walked to the second chair standing in front of Conrad's desk and sat down without taking her coat off. Calmly but efficiently, she relayed to Conrad every detail Steve had mentioned to her. Conrad listened with skilled ears. "And then," Sarah finished, taking a deep breath, "after Steve left, the redheaded mystery man appeared. In my coffee shop."

"From the look on your face, I'm guessing this man didn't have much to say?" Conrad asked.

Sarah shook her head and explained the exchange that had taken place between the red-headed man and herself. "Whoever this guy is," she said, "he's either the man who killed Sophia or he's after something related to the case."

"Maybe the book the Feds were looking for? The one Steve mentioned?" Conrad suggested.

"I was thinking the same thing," Amanda chimed in. "Sarah, you said this red-headed man told you that Sophia had to protect her brother. So maybe she had something on Gatti that made that creep back away?"

"Something on Gatti and the Feds," Conrad added. "And whoever this mystery man is wants the book for personal reasons?"

"Maybe," Sarah agreed. "I can't say he spoke with a northern accent, but I think I detected a hint of Brooklyn in his tone...faint, but there. I'm wondering if this man is part of the Sarti Family?"

Conrad drained his coffee. "This man has been in town a while," he said, tossing the paper cup into the metal trash can sitting beside his desk. "Why didn't he leave after Sophia was killed?"

"Are you suggesting Mr. Red is not the killer?" Amanda asked.

"Yes," Conrad stated honestly. "This man is searching for the same item Gatti is. He wouldn't have killed Sophia without making her confess the location of this item first."

"Good grief," Amanda fussed, "we have a major crime boss in town, a weirdo with red hair running loose, and some fussy FBI agents trying to find a book...yet, we have no killer. Need I remind you two that we have seven days before we die?"

"Whatever Sophia had kept Gatti and the Feds at bay," Conrad said.

"But," Sarah pointed out, "Sophia was AWOL for two weeks before arriving in Snow Falls. What are your thoughts on that?"

"I'm not sure yet, but my friend back in Washington is working on it for me."

"I'm hungry," Amanda announced and rubbed her

tummy. "I'm also very scared. Sarah, I want to go back to your cabin. We can get a bite to eat and brainstorm there. The last thing I want to do is get stuck in town."

Sarah listened to the snowstorm howl and scream outside the police station. "It's going to be impossible to find a killer in this storm."

"Well," Conrad said, standing up, "there is one fact we can rely on. Whoever killed Sophia wasn't after whatever Gatti, the Feds and this mystery man are—"

Bang! A bullet exploded through the window and slammed into the wall behind Conrad's head. Sarah grabbed Amanda and slung her down onto the floor as Conrad dived down behind his desk and yanked out his gun. Sarah reached down to her ankle for her own gun. "You good?" she called out to Conrad.

"I'm in the clear," he yelled, easing his eyes up over the top of his desk. "Amanda, speak to me."

"I want a raise," Amanda yelled back, keeping her head tucked under Sarah's left arm.

Sarah turned and looked at the shattered window. Powerful winds began pushing the blinds up into the air as if they were nothing more than a thin summer curtain. She had just started to get up on one knee when a second bullet announced itself screeching just past her ear. "Down!" she yelled.

"High-powered assault rifle," Conrad shouted from behind the desk. "Whoever's shooting at us knows his stuff."

Sarah heard footsteps running up to the office door and knew that Andrew was about to barge in. "Stay out!" she called, keeping her arm over Amanda's head. "Andrew, we have an active shooter outside."

"Go secure the front," Conrad yelled.

"I'm on it!" Andrew's muffled voice came through the door and Sarah heard the echo of his footsteps as he ran off.

"Amanda, crawl to the office door. We need to get out into the hallway," Sarah whispered. "Can you do that for me?"

"Los Angeles," Amanda replied in a low, tense voice, "I can crawl from here to Key West if it means staying alive."

"I hear you." Sarah helped Amanda crawl to the office door. She slowly raised her left hand, grabbed the doorknob, turned it, and eased the door open. Together, she and Amanda crawled out into the hallway. "Are you coming?" she called back to Conrad.

Conrad stared at the Venetian blinds blowing in the stormy winds. Anger ripped his chest apart. "This isn't over," he promised.

chapter six

"Come on!" Sarah yelled.

"Yeah, I'm coming." Conrad crawled out into the hallway. "There's no way Gatti is shooting at us," he said, pulling the office door shut.

"How do you know that?" Amanda asked, coming up onto her knees. "There's a crime boss in town and bullets are flying through your office window."

Sarah waited to hear a third bullet chew through Conrad's office. When the bullet didn't come, she stood up. "Let's go," she said, taking Amanda's hand and pulling her up.

"Where?"

"To the chief's office. It's time we had a little chat with him."

Conrad tucked his gun back into his shoulder holster. "Chief is out of town right now visiting his daughter. Andrew is the senior officer in charge until the chief returns from his visit."

"Speaking of Andrew, here he comes," Amanda said and nodded up the hallway.

"Tom and Edwin have the lobby secured," Andrew told Conrad. He still had his gun drawn and at the ready. "Any idea who's doing the shooting?"

"No," Conrad said tersely.

"It's got to be that Gatti guy," Andrew insisted. His voice was surprisingly calm. "Detective Spencer, who else would be sending bullets into your office?"

"It's not Gatti," Conrad growled. "Someone was sending me a message to back off, that's all."

Andrew looked at Conrad with confusion in his eyes but didn't say a word. Instead, he nodded his head and walked back to the lobby. "You were awful rude just now," Amanda told Conrad.

Ignoring her remark, Conrad turned to Sarah. "You said that Mintfield said he recognized Sophia in the grocery store, right?"

"It's possible. You said your ex-wife dyed her hair black and cut it short. Steve said the woman he saw had short black hair. What are the chances of a second woman with short black hair and a Yankee accent showing up in town?"

"And this man with the red hair and beard, he was parked outside in the parking lot that day, right?"

"Yes."

"How did this man know who Sophia was? And how did he know Sophia was hidden here in Snow Falls?"

"I don't know the answer to those questions, Conrad," Sarah confessed.

Conrad rubbed his right cheek with a frustrated hand. "Sophia goes missing for two weeks...a stranger begins to track her in town—"

"And don't forget that Mr. Red asked Steve for a spare set of keys to your ex-wife's cabin," Amanda pointed out.

"The back door to her cabin was kicked open...Sophia ends up dead."

"Conrad, I hate to jump ship on the idea that Sophia was murdered, but maybe she did freeze to death after all?" Sarah suggested. "If someone did kick the back door to her cabin open, then that means Sophia may have been scared and run out of the front door. And if she ran out into a snowstorm at night, she could have gotten lost."

Conrad continued to rub his face. "Let me chew on that idea for a while," he said slowly. He was internally struggling to dismiss the anger he was feeling and search out a logical path for his thoughts to walk on.

"We don't have a while," Amanda reminded him. "I'm with Los Angeles. I think your ex-wife got lost in the snowstorm and froze to death, too scared to return back to her cabin."

"Then why didn't she run to her truck? She had her purse, didn't she?" Conrad asked.

"Plows don't run regularly on the road she lived on. I checked," Sarah informed him. "Could have been that her truck was snowed in."

Conrad considered Sarah's argument. Understanding that his emotions were interfering with his ability to think sensibly, he drew in a deep breath and closed his eyes. "The guilt I'm feeling is tearing me apart," he confessed. "I have to take responsibility for Sophia's death. If it weren't for me...she'd still be alive. Because of me...she was brought here..." Conrad ran his hands through his hair.

Amanda shook her head and with an impatient hand, slapped Conrad across the face as hard as she could. Conrad's eyes flew open in shock. "Life is full of disappointments, New York," she scolded. "If you want to continue blaming yourself for the death of a woman who was walking down a dead-end street anyway, then go right ahead. Los Angeles and me, we have seven days to find a killer or die. And I don't think my husband wants to return from London and find his lovely wife dead, do you? So stop whining and get with the program!"

Conrad rubbed his stinging cheek. "You hit me?"

"Want me to hit you again?" Amanda asked.

Conrad stared into Amanda's fiercely caring eyes. "I get it," he promised her. "I'll get my mind back to home plate."

"Good," Amanda said. She patted his shoulder. "Because you're a good cop and I have confidence in you."

"Me, too," Sarah said. "Listen to me, okay? We have more clues than we had last night. We have a lot to go on. It's obvious Gatti thinks the killer is in town. He must think the killer knows where the book the Feds were searching for is."

"Which would explain the countdown of seven days," Conrad said, catching on to Sarah's train of thought.

"But," Sarah continued, "what if Sophia really did freeze to death and wasn't murdered? What if the Feds just wanted Gatti to believe Sophia was murdered?"

"We have a dirty Fed on our hands...or three dirty Feds," Conrad replied, looking at his office door. "It's possible that's who sent those two bullets into my office."

"As a warning to back off," Amanda said as her eyes grew wide. "Yes, I get it now. The FBI doesn't want you helping Gatti find the person who was after Sophia because they're afraid of whatever it is she had and don't want Gatti getting ahold of it. But Gatti, Mr. I'll-Smear-Your-Face-Into-The-Concrete, he's twisting our arms to help him. In the meantime, we have Mr. Red running around playing Mr. Know-It-All, the lousy bloke."

"Possibly so," Sarah congratulated Amanda on her deductions.

"We have got to find the man with the red hair," Conrad said in an urgent voice.

"He told me that he would be in touch," Sarah explained. "He also insulted my coffee, the jerk."

Conrad shoved his hands into the front pockets of his jeans. "Then all we can do is wait. The storm is predicted to grow into full force by nightfall. Tomorrow, Snow Falls will be at a complete standstill. Our job isn't going to be simple. The weather is really working against us here, guys."

"We can do this," Sarah promised, attempting to sound positive. Deep down, however, she wondered if she should run home and update her will. "Conrad, you need to ride your friend in Washington and push him to dig up everything he can. Time is really of the essence here."

Feeling exhausted from lack of sleep and too much coffee, Conrad felt a hint of irritation flash through his system. "My friend is kicking over every rock he can for us," he told Sarah in a tone that wasn't too pleasant, and then closed his eyes. "There I go again," he quickly apologized.

"And they say us women are moody," Amanda joked. She slapped him on the shoulder with a gentle hand. "You're okay, New York. Don't worry about being moody. My husband gets moody all the time. I've learned to ignore him and just smile...that drives Jack crazy."

Sarah focused on the office door again. "All is quiet," she said, attempting to force Conrad away from the negative track he was veering off onto. "Should we dare go back into your office?"

Conrad shifted his eyes to the door as well. His office was no longer a safe haven, he realized. Snow Falls was no longer a place to leave your doors unlocked at night. The small, snowy town had become a cave filled with deadly vipers waiting to strike at any second. "I'll check—"

"What's going on here?" a man's voice roared.

Sarah spun around and saw Gatti walking down the short hallway toward Conrad with his two bodyguards close behind. "What are you trying to pull?" he asked, pointing a weathered finger at Conrad.

Conrad's face turned red with anger. "Look at this," he yelled and kicked his office door open. "Someone just sent two bullets through my office window from a high-powered rifle. What am *I* trying to pull? Why don't you ask the Feds what they're trying to pull?"

Gatti walked up to Conrad's office door. Conrad moved to

the side and let Gatti view his office. "If the Feds wanted you dead, boy, you would be dead," he growled.

Sarah caught sight of Andrew at the far end of the hallway. He had his gun drawn and at the ready. "It's okay," she told him.

"Take a hike, Opie," the bodyguard in his twenties told Andrew in a sarcastic tone.

Instead of taking a hike, Andrew walked down the hallway and pointed the gun in his hand right in the face of the young bodyguard. "Listen to me," he said in a voice that made Sarah want to take cover, "this is my town, do you understand that? I know who you are, but I don't know why you're in my town. I'm hereby giving you an eviction notice. Get out of town before dark or I'm going to place you under arrest on suspicion of murder."

"What murder?" Gatti snapped at Andrew.

"The murder of an innocent woman who was found frozen to death...a woman you are acquainted with, Mr. Gatti," Andrew replied, keeping his voice firm. "The State's Attorney's Office might be very interested in knowing that a crime boss from Boston is lingering around in the town that his ex-girlfriend was brought to under the protection of the FBI. They might also be very interested in knowing how you found out the location of a woman who was in the Witness Protection Program? I know I'm mighty curious, myself."

Gatti balled his hands into furious fists. The last thing he wanted—or needed—was for a small-town cop to make trouble for him. "Don't threaten me, cop. I play rough."

Andrew kept his gun in the face of the young bodyguard and looked at Gatti. "I'm sure you do, Mr. Gatti, but up here in Alaska, we know how to play rough too. When the law fails, we take matters into our own hands. Be out of town by dark or I'm going to gather myself up an old-fashioned posse of men who tangle with hungry grizzly bears just for the fun of it."

Gatti's breathing grew faster as he realized he was outnumbered. The truth was, he was outnumbered and outflanked until he could get more of his own men situated onto the battleground. "You're a dead man," he promised Andrew.

"Mr. Gatti," Andrew said, nodding his head at Conrad, "you have the right to remain silent. Anything you say or do..."

Gatti looked at Conrad. Conrad whipped out his gun and pointed it at him. "You threatened a cop in front of three witnesses," he told Gatti. "You may kill me in seven days, Gatti...but I'm not going to stand by and let you threaten a good man. Put your hands behind your back."

The bodyguard in his forties reached for his gun. Out of instinct, Sarah reached for her ankle, yanked her gun out of the holster, and pointed it at the bodyguard. "Freeze," she yelled.

"Do what the cop says," Gatti told his bodyguard in a low growl. He narrowed his eyes at Conrad. "You're being very stupid. I came here because I thought you sent someone to shoot at my limo. I would have walked away after seeing your office. Now, it's personal."

"It's always been personal," Conrad said. "Deep down, Sophia loved me and I loved her. But you were just her toy, Gatti, and nothing more. Now get your hands behind your back."

"And you two drop your guns," Andrew warned Gatti's bodyguards.

"Do it," Gatti ordered. "Pick your headstone, boy," he warned Conrad as he put his wrists behind his back and turned around.

Sarah waited until Gatti's two bodyguards disarmed themselves. Sensing Amanda staring at her, she looked at her friend. "What?"

"You were awesome!" Amanda exclaimed.

"Freeze...pow...wham! Policewoman at your service. I can't wait to tell Jack about this."

Sarah looked over at Conrad. He winked at her. "Once a cop, always a cop," he said proudly.

"You're all dead men walking," Gatti warned.

Amanda, sick of being threatened, threw her hands up at Gatti. "Oh, go eat a poisoned cannoli." She walked away toward the front lobby, mumbling to herself. "Bald-headed bloke thinks he can scare me, he has another thing coming..."

Sarah and Conrad stared at each other with uncertainty. Outside, the snow continued to fall, and the storm grew stronger.

chapter seven

"Gatti won't make bail until he sees Judge Fleishman," Conrad told Sarah as they sat at the table in her kitchen. "Today is Thursday, and the judge won't be back in town till Monday. Until then, Gatti will be sitting on ice along with his two thugs."

"That's good then, right?" Amanda asked, munching on a turkey sandwich.

"Actually, it is," Conrad said. He looked down at the half-eaten grilled cheese sandwich sitting on his plate. "Whoever sent those bullets into my office unintentionally did us a huge favor."

"Gatti's temper did us a huge favor," Sarah added, taking a bite of leftover shepherd's pie. "He was stupid to threaten a cop in front of reliable witnesses."

"Unless..." Amanda began as a sudden thought ran through her mind. "Say, do you guys think maybe Gatti *wanted* to be arrested?"

Conrad looked across the kitchen table at Sarah. He shrugged his shoulders. "It's a thought," he admitted.

Sarah nodded. "We did find his limo with the front right wheel shot out," she said. "But why would Gatti allow himself to be arrested? He's not the type of man to run scared."

"I'm not sure...assuming Gatti intentionally threatened Andrew with the purpose of being arrested," Conrad confessed. He began to speak again when a hard knock struck the back door. Conrad exploded to his feet and pulled out his gun.

Sarah reached out and grabbed her own gun, which she had placed beside the dinner plate. "Amanda—"

"I know." Amanda quickly crawled under the kitchen table.

"Ready?" Sarah whispered to Conrad. He nodded his head and dropped down onto one knee. "Who is it?" Sarah called out.

"The man who knows the truth," a voice called back.

"It's him, the red-headed man," Sarah whispered.

"Open the door," Conrad ordered, keeping his gun aimed at the back door.

Sarah reluctantly walked to the back door, unlocked the deadbolt, and pulled the door open. Freezing winds and heavy snow immediately slapped her in the face. "Inside," she told the man standing there, covered with snow.

"It isn't a night fit for man or beast," the red-headed man replied as Sarah moved away and he stepped through the back door. "You can put your guns away," he raised his hands as he spotted Conrad. "I'm not here to harm anyone."

"Then why are you here?" Sarah asked.

The man turned and closed the back door behind him. "Gatti is in jail," he said calmly. He began stomping snow off a pair of black boots. "He was smart."

"Who are you?" Conrad demanded. "I want a name and I want it right now."

"Call me...Hank."

"I want a real name."

"Hank will have to do."

"Okay... 'Hank,'" Sarah said, putting her gun back down on the kitchen table, "how did you find my home address?"

Hank looked at the table but didn't show any signs that he was aware Amanda was hiding under it. "Gatti was smart," he repeated. "May I sit down and have a cup of coffee?"

"Sit down," Sarah acquiesced.

Conrad waited until Hank sat down before retaking his own seat. "How do you know Gatti?" he asked.

"Gatti and I are old friends," Hank explained. "But for now, let's focus on Sophia, okay? You see, I came here to protect her. I failed."

"I'm all ears." Conrad laid his gun in his lap. "Talk to me."

Sarah poured Hank a cup of coffee and brought it to him. "Steve Mintfield informed me that you became...temperamental with him when he refused to give you a set of keys to the rental cabin Sophia was living in. Yet you seem so calm and mild-tempered now. Care to explain?" she asked.

"I was having a very bad day," Hank replied, taking his cup of coffee from her. "Sophia...so stubborn. She refused to listen to me. I knew whatever time I had was running out. I admit it was foolish to annoy Mr. Mintfield, but I was desperate."

Conrad watched Hank take a sip of coffee. The man's coat was soaked with snow, along with the black ski cap he was wearing on his head and the black gloves covering his hands. But even without examining the man's winter clothing, it was obvious from his red, frozen face that he had been out in the storm for a long period of time. "How long have you been standing at the back door listening?"

"Long enough to know that it was time to choose sides in this mess."

Sarah sat down. "How did you find my home address?" she asked again.

"You can find anyone's home address online," Hank

informed her, sounding disappointed. "Detective Garland, you should know that."

Conrad gave Sarah a strange look. He wasn't sure why she had allowed her critical thinking skills to appear weak. "Okay," Sarah said, switching gears, "where are you staying, Hank?"

"My location must remain a secret," Hank warned her. "I may have chosen sides tonight, but we are far from friends. Is that clear?"

"Clear," Sarah said.

Conrad sat still for a few seconds and focused on the snowstorm outside. "Nothing is moving out there," he told Hank. "We barely made it through the snow to get here, and that was over three hours ago. By now the roads are completely crippled."

"I have a snowmobile," Hank informed him. "Is that a crime?"

"Where did you park your snowmobile?" Conrad asked.

"None of your business." Hank sipped on his coffee. "The local 'Tin Badge' station has a few snowmobiles at their disposal, though. If you want to go for a ride in the snow, use one of the snowmobiles the poor taxpayers were forced to pay for."

Conrad nodded. "Maybe I will if the need arises."

Sarah studied Hank's face. Snow was still stuck to his beard. "You've been watching everyone today, haven't you?"

"I saw the man who decided to cost the taxpayers more money by shooting through Detective Spencer's office window, yes." Hank looked down at Amanda's half-eaten turkey sandwich. "May I?" he asked.

"Go ahead," Sarah said.

Hank grabbed the sandwich with hungry fingers and tore into it like a starving animal. "The man that fired the two bullets through your office window," he told Conrad with his mouth full of turkey, "is an FBI agent. But you already know that."

"I kinda figured," Conrad admitted. "The Feds are searching for whatever Sophia had on them."

"A book," Sarah added.

Hank took another sip of hot coffee and continued to work on the sandwich. "The Feds didn't kill Sophia, but they wanted her dead," he went on. Sarah noticed that he ignored her book comment and wondered if he knew anything. "Sophia was foolish to call Gatti. She attempted to make a deal with him." Hank looked at Conrad, then back to Sarah, and allowed time for his statement to sink in. "Sophia was preparing to run."

"Who killed her?" Conrad demanded, feeling his patience growing thin. "Just tell me who killed my ex-wife and we can handle the minor details later."

"Who killed Sophia?" Hank asked contemplatively, finishing off the sandwich and then sliding his gaze over to Sarah's shepherd's pie. Sarah slid her plate over to him. "Thank you," he said and dug into the food. "Who killed Sophia?" he repeated. "That's the one question that's keeping me alive."

Conrad snatched his coffee cup off the table. "Take a hike," he told Hank and drained the cup. "Go play games with Gatti or the Feds."

"Gatti wants you dead because of what Sophia told him about you," Hank warned. "She wanted revenge on you, Detective."

Sarah raised a hand at Conrad and shook her head. "Please, Conrad, let him talk," she pleaded. She turned to face Hank. "What did Sophia tell Gatti?" she asked in a concerned voice.

Hank was still eating the shepherd's pie. "That Detective Spencer knew the identity of the man who was sent to this snowy little village to kill her." He took another bite. "Sophia made Gatti promise that if anything happened to her...if she ended up dead...that he would find Detective Spencer and force him to track down her killer."

"Gatti's given each of us seven days to live," Sarah told Hank.

"That's because seven days is all the time Gatti has left to live, technically speaking." Hank finished off the shepherd's pie and next grabbed Conrad's half-eaten grilled cheese. "In seven days, the man who was sent to kill Sophia is going to make her little diary public. Yes, Detective Spencer, I'm fully aware of the diary your ex-wife was keeping."

"Sophia always did like to walk on the edge," Conrad sighed.

"The man who was sent to kill Sophia has gathered all of his enemies into one place to kill them, is that it?" Sarah asked.

Hank shifted his eyes to Sarah. "You're smart," he said in a curious voice. "Maybe too smart."

"We'll see," Sarah said wryly.

"Does that mean Detective Garland is right?" Conrad asked. "Is Sophia's killer gathering his enemies into one place?"

"Not his enemies...Sophia's enemies," Hank corrected. "Sophia couldn't have known that you, of all people, would relocate to Alaska to track down her killer. She manipulated Gatti into forcing you to come here. But you were way ahead of the game, Detective Spencer. Now, all the pawns are on the chessboard, and the man Sophia so desperately feared is ready to play his deadly game."

"And you want to make sure that you teach us how to checkmate in three moves, is that it?" Conrad asked. "While you remain the strong Queen?"

Hank finished the grilled cheese sandwich and wiped his mouth with his coat sleeve. "I have to stay alive," he told Conrad in a serious tone.

"You seem to know a lot about the woman I used to be married to," Conrad said suspiciously. "I've never seen you before, and Sophia never made any mention of you, either. Who are you? I want answers."

"In time," Hank replied and gazed into the rich brown liquid. "As I said, Gatti and I are old friends, but not in the way you think. I was employed with The Boston Globe for a number of years. During my time there as a reporter, I became well-acquainted with Gatti and his crime organization. I was young at the time, fresh out of college, and very foolish. I was of the irritating mindset that I could take on the world and win. I learned very fast that the world was cold, deadly, crooked, and cruel, and that I was not going to go twelve rounds with anyone and come out holding my hands up in victory."

"Gatti slapped you around some, huh?" Conrad deduced. "You decided to make a name for yourself and went after the biggest player in town, and you learned the hard way that the big boys play rough."

Hank fidgeted with his coffee cup. "Let's just say that Gatti let me know that unless the articles I submitted to the paper were written to his satisfaction...my career would come to a sudden and painful end."

Sarah soaked in Hank's facial expressions, tones, body language, and eye movements. "You didn't like Gatti threatening you, right?"

Hank looked over his shoulder and focused on the back door. The storm was howling and screaming outside, daring him to leave the cabin. "I was always hot-tempered," he told Sarah. "As a child, I saw my old man bully my mother...he was a horrible bully. When I grew strong enough, I began defending my mother, which only made matters worse. The more I defended her, the madder I became inside. Before I knew it, I began bullying kids at my school." Hank refocused his attention back on Sarah. "My temper never simmered down, and to this day it takes a great deal of inner strength to control it. When Gatti tied my hands and prevented me from writing articles, I snapped and went after the man in full force."

"But not with the pen," Sarah inferred.

Hank shook his head. "I began watching Gatti, studying the man, investigating his actions, words, personal behaviors. I studied him the way a scientist studies a mouse in a maze."

"When does Sophia come into the picture?" Conrad asked impatiently.

"Sophia came into the game the day I saw her get out of a limo holding onto Gatti's arm. Oh, she was a beautiful woman. Young, daring, challenging...she was just the ticket I needed to destroy Gatti. This was before Sophia met you, of course."

"Get on with it," Conrad ordered. "It's getting late."

"Yes, it's getting very late," Hank agreed. He caught Sarah reading his eyes. "I took a chance," he said, as he shifted his uncomfortable gaze away from Sarah, "and approached Sophia one afternoon while she was carrying groceries home to her apartment from Mac's Grocery Store. She had her arms full and was in need of assistance. The right moment had finally presented itself, and I moved in. To be honest, because Sophia was so beautiful, I was a little nervous, but I knew the time to act had come." Hank finished his coffee and asked Sarah for a refill.

Sarah took his cup and refilled it with hot coffee. "Here you go."

"Thank you." He took the cup. "Sophia wasn't very accepting of my chivalry," he continued. "She had a very smart, sharp mouth on her. However, I threw my charm into overdrive and insisted that I help carry the groceries. She reluctantly agreed because she had two gallons of milk weighing down one of the brown paper bags in her arms."

"Sophia loved her milk," Conrad whispered to himself.

With sadness in his eyes, he looked down at the gun in his lap.

"Yes, she did," Hank confirmed. "I walked Sophia to her apartment, and when we arrived I dared to ask her for a date. I expected her to slap me in the face. Instead, she pointed to a little coffee shop across the street from her apartment and agreed to have coffee with me after she put away her groceries. I was shocked, but I didn't show it. Why would such a beautiful woman, one who initially told me to get lost, suddenly agree to have coffee with me?"

"Sophia never wanted to owe anyone anything," Conrad explained. "You did her a favor, so she did you a favor."

"I learned that fact later on," Hank said. "Anyway, we had coffee and I really poured on the charm. I didn't know it then, but at the time Gatti was pressuring Sophia to marry him. She wasn't interested. But I soon learned that Sophia was going to use me to help her escape Gatti's clutches."

"How?" Conrad insisted.

"Sophia was sharp. She did some checking and found out that I worked for the Globe. With that truth in hand, she pushed me into a corner. She told me that she would turn over damaging information on Gatti only if I agreed to publish the information in the Globe. But I had other plans. I hired a private detective to take photos of us when we were out on our dates...one picture was taken of us kissing." Hank looked down at his hands. "I really did care about Sophia. I guess I...loved her. But my rage against Gatti was so intense that I couldn't see that she was nothing more than a scared little girl wanting someone to love her."

"Skip the dramatics," Conrad snapped. "I was married to the woman."

Hank looked up sharply. "Well, she's dead now," he snapped back.

There was a pause.

"Sophia dripped information on Gatti to me in slow,

painful stages. She was scared. She didn't trust anyone, not even me. She threatened to have Gatti kill me if I betrayed her. Anyway, long story short, the day came when Sophia finally disclosed enough information to damage Gatti's reputation and cause him severe legal troubles. But by that time...I had fallen in love with Sophia and realized I couldn't use her to get my revenge on Gatti. So, I decided to publish what I had on the worm and make a run for it with Sophia. Only..."

"Only Gatti found out and cut you off at the path," Conrad reasoned.

Hank slowly nodded his head. "Two of his henchmen ambushed me outside of Sophia's apartment one night and drove me to a warehouse. Gatti was waiting for me, and so was Sophia. She begged Gatti to spare my life, but Gatti wouldn't listen. He..." Hank paused.

"What?" Conrad asked. "What did he do to you?"

"It was winter," Hank said in a pained voice. "Gatti had me tied up and thrown into the Charles River. When my feet touched the bottom of the river, I sprang myself upward and managed to break the surface to get air before sinking back down. Because it was the middle of the night and freezing cold, the two morons who threw me in were too busy getting their boat back to shore and didn't see me." Hank drew in a deep breath. "Little by little, I kept moving toward the shore, going up and down, up and down like a spring, catching small doses of air before going back under the water. Finally...I made it to the shore."

Sarah stared into Hank's face. She saw revenge flash through his eyes. "You must have been frozen stiff."

"I was too angry to notice how cold I was," Hank confessed. "But I knew that going after Gatti again would certainly be the last thing I ever did, so I played dead. I hid in the shadows and watched." Hank looked at Conrad. "I watched you play a deadly game. I also watched Sophia fall in love with you."

Conrad stood up. "Hit the fast-forward button. How did you end up here in Alaska?"

"The night Sophia was to leave for Alaska, she was staying at a little motel outside Newark, right?" Hank asked.

"The Bright Night Inn," Conrad confirmed, impatiently tapping his fingers.

"The FBI agents in charge of watching Sophia's room weren't too sharp," Hank explained. "I slipped up on the car they were sitting in...very easily, I might add. Only, my gun wasn't a real gun, just a tranquilizer that worked very well." Hank smiled for the first time that evening at the memory. "With my foes taken care of, I knocked on Sophia's door."

Conrad felt like punching Hank in the face. "How did she react?"

"Shocked, of course," Hank said. "I didn't stay for very long. I told Sophia how I felt about her and gave her my private number. Before I left, I asked her to give me the private diary I knew she'd been keeping. She refused. I explained to her that I was going after Gatti, but still...she refused. What else could I do? I left."

"Just like that, huh?" Conrad asked.

"Sophia had a plan up her sleeve and she wasn't going to let me ruin it. And whatever her plan was involved Gatti," Hank said firmly. "I thought... I believed...that when Sophia saw me alive, that she would surely help me. I was wrong."

"You attacked two FBI agents," Sarah said. "I'm sure Sophia had her reasons for being cautious."

"Reasons not concerning the Feds," Hank replied darkly.

"When did Sophia call you?" Conrad asked.

"When she realized that she was going to die," Hank said, rising from his chair.

Sarah rubbed the tip of her nose as her mind formed

different questions. "Why would Sophia tell Gatti that Detective Spencer knew the identity of her future killer?"

"Enough for tonight," Hank said. He walked toward the back door. "I'll come back tomorrow and we'll talk more."

"One more question, tough guy," Conrad stopped him. "Sophia disappeared for two weeks before arriving in Alaska. Any idea where she went?"

"Haven't got a clue." Hank opened the back door. "Like I said, Gatti was smart to get himself arrested. The Feds are getting desperate," he said as the icy winds outside hit his face. "Tomorrow, we'll earn our checkmate."

Without warning, in one swift movement, Conrad ran to the back door, grabbed Hank, and slammed him down onto the kitchen floor. "You killed her, didn't you?" he yelled, throwing his gun into Hank's face. "You were the one who kicked open her back door. You wanted her diary to destroy Gatti, and once you got the diary, you killed her. Sophia knew your plan, didn't she?"

"Calm down, Conrad," Sarah pleaded.

Hank stared up into Conrad's furious eyes. "I loved Sophia," he replied in a surprisingly calm voice, although he was starting to see red. "If I wanted to kill Sophia, I would have done it the night I visited her at the Bright Night Inn. Tonight, I chose my side... Sophia was forced to choose her side, and she chose to return to Gatti. Maybe you'd better ask yourself why?"

"Where was she for those missing two weeks?!" Conrad yelled in Hank's face. "Where did the Feds take her?"

Hank paused for a moment. "Do you really want to know the truth?"

"Yes."

He took a deep breath. "They tortured her for two weeks because of me," Hank yelled. "The FBI tortured Sophia because they believed she'd passed off her diary to me because I shot their buddies with a tranquilizer gun and tied them up."

"Sophia didn't call you because she wanted your help," Conrad growled, "she called you to turn you over to the Feds."

"Oh, the games people play," Hank replied. "Now either arrest me or let me up."

"You wanted her diary, but Sophia knew if you took it, she would be dead. It was only her diary that was keeping her alive," Conrad said, rapidly putting the pieces of the puzzle together in his mind. "You managed to get to the diary, didn't you?"

"Get off of me," Hank warned.

"Sophia was going to turn you over to the Feds to save her life while running to Gatti to get him to come and rescue her and hide her. Gatti would never hurt Sophia. He may have threatened her life, but everyone with enough sense to tie their shoes knows that Gatti never would've hurt her. The Feds are after Sophia's diary, and the person who was sent to kill Sophia has her diary, and that person is you!"

Hank's eyes were cold and unreadable. "You think you have it all figured out, don't you? But you're missing one important fact."

"What?"

"I don't have Sophia's diary. The man who was sent to kill Sophia has her diary." Hank looked over at Sarah. "Tell him I'm not the killer."

"I really don't think Hank is the killer," Sarah told Conrad. "Let him up. We have no charges to hold him on."

Conrad stared deep into Hank's eyes. "I'm going to catch you."

"We'll see," Hank shoved Conrad off of him and stood up. "I'll be in touch," he said to Sarah, and then escaped out the back door.

Conrad slammed the door shut. "What are your thoughts?" he asked Sarah.

"This," Amanda said from beneath the kitchen table. Sarah lifted up the tablecloth. Amanda smiled and held up a key. "So I learned to pick pockets as a teenager. Every girl hangs out with the wrong crowd at some point in her life."

Sarah took the key. "It's the key to the snowmobile," she realized. She tossed the key to Conrad. "Amanda, you are my hero."

Conrad caught the key and examined it. "When Hank realizes he doesn't have the key, he'll pay us a second visit. Let's get ready for him."

"Hank isn't the man we're after," Sarah reminded him as she helped Amanda up. "But," she added, "Hank *is* after the man sent to kill Sophia. This man has Sophia's diary. Only a man would call a diary a book. When Steve said the FBI agents were fussing about finding a book, I considered the possibility the book in question was a diary."

"So who is the man that was sent to kill Sophia?" Amanda asked.

Conrad slid the snowmobile key into his front right pocket and focused on Sarah. "Detective Garland, who has Sophia's diary?" he asked calmly.

"A man who wants every one of Sophia's enemies dead," Sarah answered. "Conrad, I'm going to need you to make a call to New York and perform a check for me. Can you do that?"

Conrad nodded his head. "Write down what you need, partner." He glanced at the back door. "And make it quick. Our friend will be returning soon."

Sarah stared at the back door. "Hank is desperate and probably running very low on funds. You saw the way he ate our food. I don't believe he's a threat, Conrad. The man just wants revenge on Gatti and the FBI agent who was with Gatti on the night he was ambushed in front of Sophia's apartment."

"So Gatti and the Feds know Hank is alive...and they think he has the diary?" Conrad began pacing the kitchen.

"They know he's alive," Sarah agreed. "And most likely, yes, they believe Hank has the diary. But Hank said Gatti was smart to get himself arrested...guys, maybe it wasn't the Feds who sent us those two bullets. Conrad, get ready to make that call."

Conrad quickly held up a hand. "Hold it," he said, "if the Feds didn't send us those gift-wrapped bullets, then who do you think..." He stopped talking. His eyes went wide and then narrowed.

"What?" Amanda begged. "Speak up, man. Time is ticking away and my Jack is going to be returning home next week. It would be nice if he found his wife breathing and alive."

Conrad bit down on his lower lip, nodded his head, and dashed to the back door. Before Sarah could stop him, he grabbed his coat off the coat rack and raced outside into the snowstorm. "Conrad!" Sarah yelled, running to the open back door. "Conrad!"

"That man is crazy," Amanda cried, hurrying over to the back door and peering into the dark, stormy night. Shielding her eyes against the screaming winds that were reaching into the warm kitchen, she searched for Conrad. "There," she said and pointed to a shadowy figure disappearing into the woods.

Sarah spotted Conrad struggling through the knee-deep snow at an impressive speed. "He's following Hanks boot tracks," she observed. "The wind and snow haven't completely covered them yet."

"What's the plan?" Amanda asked, fearing that Conrad would die in a snowstorm.

Feeling the winds cut into her face with razor-sharp claws,

Sarah slowly pushed the door closed. "It's foolish to go out into the storm," she told Amanda, "and that's why you're staying inside."

"Oh, no." Amanda shook her head. "If you're going out into the storm, so am I," she informed Sarah stubbornly. "I'll get our coats."

"Listen," Sarah begged, "I need to go alone. I love you dearly, June Bug, but...you'll just get in my way. Please, stay here in the cabin. If I'm not back by sun-up, call Andrew and have him send out a search party."

Amanda searched Sarah's eyes, struggling to see what her best friend was thinking. "Is this a cop thing?" she asked.

Sarah took her coat off the rack and put it on. "Yes," she said, pulling her hat and gloves out of the left pocket of her coat.

Amanda watched Sarah put on her gloves and pink snow cap. "The winds are going to really chew you up," she said in a worried voice. "What chance do you have in this storm? Please, stay inside where it's safe and warm."

Sarah opened the back door once more and looked out into the dark snow. "Sophia's brother is out there in the snow," she said, narrowing her eyes. "There's another creepy snowman out there in those woods, and this time, it's after Conrad instead of me. Stay here."

Before Amanda could say another word, Sarah rushed out into the snow. With shaky hands, Amanda reached out and reluctantly closed the door behind her. "It's going to be a very long night," she sighed, and began praying for Sarah's safety.

Knowing that a flashlight would easily give away her position, Sarah depended on her sharp eyes to carry her through the snow. Keeping her sight directly on the snow-covered ground, she carefully followed Conrad's boot tracks, which the winds and snow were quickly destroying. After working her way to the end of the backyard, Sarah paused and glanced over her shoulder. The cabin sat behind her like a warm lighthouse begging her to return. "I have to fight for Conrad," she whispered through shivering lips. Knowing that the winds would cut her in half if she stayed immobile for too long, Sarah bravely looked forward, examined the dark woods standing before her, and cautiously stepped into the mouth of a horrible, vicious snowman.

chapter eight

"Keep moving forward," Sarah said through chattering teeth as she maneuvered her way past one dark snowy tree after another. The tall trees permitted some relief from the winds and snow, allowing a longer lifespan for Conrad's tracks. "Hank wouldn't have parked his snowmobile too far from the cabin..."

Feeling her feet becoming hard blocks of ice, Sarah paused. The snow was deeper in the woods than in her backyard. The air was much colder and much more deadly, too. Even though the trees were offering mild protection from the winds and snow, they were also acting as an icy canvas, holding in the cold. Looking upward, Sarah studied the dark mouths of the trees with scared eyes. "If I'm not careful, I'll get myself lost out here," she worried as every fiber of her being begged her to turn around and return to the cabin. "I have to keep moving...once a cop, always a cop," she said determinedly.

Lifting her gloved hands up to her ears, Sarah began to move forward again. Walking past one snowy tree and then another, following Conrad's tracks, she tried to think but found that any thought she formed quickly dropped from her mind into the snow. It was taking every ounce of her energy just to walk forward through the dark woods, and Sarah knew that she had to shut down her mind and allow her instincts to take over. Stepping through the deep snow, one miserable, frozen step at a time, she pushed her body forward.

Bang! A gunshot rang out not more than twenty feet ahead of her, Sarah immediately stopped walking and dropped down onto one knee. Pulling out her gun, she studied the darkness.

"Get down!" she faintly heard Conrad's voice yell. "Get down now! Face down!"

"Don't shoot!" Hank's frantic voice raced over the winds.

"He's caught up with Hank." Relieved to hear Conrad's voice, Sarah began to stand up. But as she did, a vicious hand exploded out of the darkness and knocked her unconscious with a broken tree limb. As she fell face first into the snow, Sarah drifted off into a cold darkness...drifting...drifting...so much snow...so much wind... *Why did my husband divorce me?... What did I do wrong?*...so much snow...

"Sleep tight," a deadly voiced hissed at Sarah, then slithered off into the dark snow.

Two hours later, Sarah woke up on her couch with a white bandage wrapped around her head. Amanda was standing by the fireplace sipping on a cup of coffee. "June...Bug..." Sarah struggled to speak as her eyes fluttered open. Incredible pain immediately punished her for daring to speak. "My...head..."

Amanda set her coffee mug down on the wooden mantle and ran to Sarah. "You're alive," she said happily. Kneeling down next to Sarah, she lovingly hugged her best friend's arm. "I was afraid you might die."

"I..." Sarah tried to speak as her head exploded in more pain. "My head..."

"You have a concussion...I think. Some coward hit you in

the back of the head with a tree limb. I found pieces of bark in your hair."

"You...found..." Sarah repeated, confused.

"After you ran out to play in the snow, I decided to wait in the kitchen for about twenty minutes and then...well, you're my best friend...I couldn't just stand around and do nothing," Amanda explained.

"You went out into the snow after me?" Sarah moaned as her eyesight swayed back into a cloud of blurriness.

"And it's a good thing that I did," Amanda fussed. She let go of Sarah's arm and, with the manner of a loving nurse who was not pleased with her patient, checked Sarah's head bandage. "At first I thought the winds were going to kill me," she confessed. "There I was, little bitty me, walking through the big dark woods, barely—and I do mean barely—able to follow your boot tracks. And what happened, you might ask? Well, I'll tell you what happened: I found you lying face down in the snow, like a drowned woman floating face down in a pool."

"You...saved my life," Sarah said gratefully. "June...Bug...my hero."

Amanda quickly took her hands away from Sarah's head and wiped at the warm tears that had begun to stream down her cheeks. "I was very scared," she admitted. "Los Angeles...what happened? Who hurt you?"

Sarah struggled to focus but then dropped away into a warm darkness. Gray beams of light coming in from the living room windows woke her up six hours later. "Amanda?" she asked.

"Right here," Amanda said. She was cuddled up in a warm blanket in the sitting chair next to the couch. "The storm is worse, Los Angeles. Nothing is moving out there."

To Sarah's relief, her eyes were no longer blurry and the pain in her head had become tolerable. "You went out into the snow after me..."

"Don't remind me," Amanda yawned. "Try and rest. I've been taking little cat naps. I managed to get some aspirin into you an hour ago. You can have another dose in three hours."

"Is Conrad—" Sarah began to speak but stopped when someone knocked on the front door.

Amanda threw the warm blanket covering her to the floor and jumped to her feet like a cat that had just been doused in a bucket of icy water. "Who is it!" she yelled.

"Please, let me in," a woman's voice begged.

Amanda crept over to the front door. "Be careful," Sarah begged, forcing her body into a sitting position.

"Who are you?" Amanda yelled through the front door.

"My name is Sophia," the woman standing out in the storm answered. "Please, I'm in horrible trouble and I need Detective Garland's help."

"She's alive? Let her in," Sarah instructed. She began to reach for her gun but found her ankle holster empty. "My gun..." Images of the dark woods flooded into her mind. "I had my gun in my hand when..."

"Calm down," Amanda begged Sarah.

"Please," the woman named Sophia cried from outside, "I'm freezing out here!"

"Let her in," Sarah ordered.

"Jack is never going to let me stay home alone again," Amanda fussed as she unlocked the front door. "Here we go," she said uncertainly, and she pulled the front door open.

A beautiful woman with dark black hair, covered with snow from top to bottom, appeared. "May I come inside?" she begged.

"Hurry," Amanda said. She pulled the woman inside and slammed the front door shut. "Go to the fireplace."

Sophia ran to the fireplace and began warming her bare hands. She wasn't wearing a coat or a hat. An oversized gray sweater and a pair of blue ski pants tucked into black snow boots were the only items covering Sophia's body. "You're supposed to be dead," Sarah whispered, placing her left hand on the back of her head.

Sophia looked at Sarah. The woman's beauty was mesmerizing. Her eyes resembled blue diamonds that could cut through the heart of any man. "I did what I had to do," she said in a sharp voice that quickly turned into sorrow. "It was Frank's idea to hire that poor woman."

"Where is Conrad?" Sarah demanded.

"Frank has him...he has Mitch, too."

"Who?" Amanda asked.

"Mitch is Hank," Sarah moaned as a sharp pain lunged through her head.

Sophia continued to warm her hands. "Please," she pleaded with Sarah, "you have to help me. Agent McQuire is going to kill us all if we don't stop him."

"Agent McQuire is the FBI agent who was with Gatti the day they decided to throw Mitch into the river, right?" Sarah asked.

"I begged them to spare Mitch's life... Mitch isn't a bad guy, honestly. I admit that I manipulated him. Gatti threatened to kill my brother if I ever tried to leave him. I had to create a way to destroy Gatti, and Mitch was my chance."

"Your brother set this all up, didn't he?" Sarah asked.

"Yes," Sophia admitted regretfully. "Frank thought of a plan to get Gatti, McQuire and that lying ex-husband of mine into one place. We knew Conrad would figure it out that the woman who died in my place was a fake...he had to die."

"Only you didn't want Conrad to die, is that it? That man has been tormenting himself over your death," Sarah said accusingly.

"Who knew that jerk loved me that much?" Sophia exclaimed. "I went behind my brother's back and called Mitch. I begged for his help in return for my diary. That's all Mitch wanted anyway."

"Maybe not," Sarah told her, "but keep talking."

"I asked Mitch to help me escape from my brother. I love my brother, I really do...but he's a deadly man, Detective Garland. If he kills Gatti, do you know what will happen?"

"A mafia war," Sarah said.

Sophia nodded her head. "Frank was going to make it look like Sarti killed Gatti and that the Feds were involved. Conrad...was personal."

"Mitch didn't play your game, did he?" Sarah asked.

"Mitch refused to help me unless I gave him the diary up front," Sophia confessed. "He wasn't the same Mitch I knew from Boston...he had changed...become hard...dangerous...empty. I knew from the moment I saw his eyes that I had made a horrible mistake asking for his help. I begged Mitch to leave, but he threatened to go to my brother and expose my betrayal...so I went to Frank and confessed everything."

"What happened?" Amanda asked, still standing at the front door.

"Natalie Delanie was summoned," Sophia said shamefully. "Frank had been making trips to visit Natalie in Fairbanks. He hired her to come to my cabin and pretend to be me...first to lure Mitch in and kill him...and second...to kill her in order to lure Gatti, McQuire, and Conrad to Alaska."

Sarah forced her legs to work. She stood up, eased her way over to the fireplace and looked Sophia in her eyes. "You wanted Mitch to kill your brother."

Sophia stared into a pair of brilliant eyes. Unable to look away, she slowly nodded her head. "Frank is insane. He wants to kill Gatti and Mr. Sarti and take over both families. McQuire is a dirty Fed, and he has a lot of dirty friends under him. With McQuire out of the way, Frank will be able to expose the dishonest Feds to whoever cares."

"And Frank intends to kill you, too, right?"

Sophia couldn't look away from Sarah. "My diary...that's all he cares about. My diary is keeping me alive."

"Does your brother have your diary?" Amanda asked.

"No one does," Sophia replied. She pulled up her dress sleeve and exposed her left arm, revealing ugly scars. "For two weeks McQuire tried to get me to give him my diary. I refused. He put me here and threatened to kill me if I left. My Subaru has a tracking device on it and my cabin is bugged. I have one credit card, which McQuire tracks."

"You were put on ice," Sarah said.

"Yes. But Frank is smart. He found me by bribing a dirty Fed."

Sarah walked away. "Keep talking."

Sophia pulled her sleeve down. "Mitch must have become suspicious because he stopped making contact with me. So Frank started sending Natalie into town to see if Mitch would take the bait. Mitch is a smart guy, though. Anyway, on the day the storm hit last month, Frank sent Natalie to the grocery store hoping Mitch would make contact. While Natalie was gone, Frank became very drunk on vodka. When Natalie returned from the grocery store with only a single bag of groceries and no Mitch, Frank exploded."

"Of course, he did," Sarah said, "because you made your brother believe that Mitch had your diary."

"You're a very smart woman." Sophia looked at the fire playing in the fireplace. "Yes, I told Frank that Mitch had stolen my diary. I hid my diary under the fireplace floor...no one thought to look there. It was very difficult to break a hole through the floor, but I did. I guess my repair job wasn't the greatest, but when I burned a few fires, no one could tell that a hole had been dug."

"Except Steve Mintfield," Sarah said. "Sophia, you don't have your diary now, do you?" she asked urgently. "Your diary is missing."

"Yes," Sophia said in a scared voice. "When Natalie returned to my cabin with no word on Mitch, Frank tied her up and marched her into the woods at gunpoint. I begged him to spare her life...I couldn't go through with his plan.

Frank threatened to kill me if I didn't shut up. I...stayed at my cabin. When night came, Frank kicked open the back door and ordered me out. He drove me to a rental cabin he was renting under a false name and tied me up. For three days Frank kept leaving...on the third day he came back and told me Natalie was dead."

"Poor woman," Amanda said sadly.

"Frank made an anonymous call to the Park Ranger Service," Sophia continued. "After he made the call, he untied me and threatened to kill me if I didn't leave town. He shoved some money, a fake ID, and a plane ticket in my pocket and told me to fly back to New York."

"You didn't leave, obviously," Sarah said.

"I did leave," Sophia confessed. "I left my diary in its hiding place and flew to New York. But when I had a close friend of mine check on Conrad and she found out the guy had been transferred to Snow Falls, I knew I had to come back. Conrad betrayed me...and we're over...but I still care about him. I'll never love the jerk in the same way again, but I can't let Frank kill him."

"You just tried to save Conrad, didn't you?" Sarah began looking for her coat.

"Frank has Conrad and Mitch at his rental cabin. He's going for Gatti when night falls. McQuire will be here tomorrow," Sophia explained. "Gatti thought he was smart putting himself behind bars until McQuire arrives, but Frank will get to him."

"Frank was the one who shot at us yesterday, right?" Sarah asked, grabbing her coat.

"Yes."

"Amanda, I'm going to pay Steve Mintfield a visit. You stay here with Sophia." Sarah gingerly slid her coat on over her bruised arms. "Sophia, where is Frank's rental cabin located?"

Sophia looked down at her feet as she told Sarah the

location. "I tried to save Conrad. Honestly, I did," she said. "Frank caught me and tried to kill me...Conrad saved my life. He tripped Frank as he came at me, giving me enough time to escape out the front door."

"Watch her," Sarah ordered Amanda. "If she tries to leave, deck her in the face."

"You bet I will," Amanda said and pointed at the couch. "Park it, sister."

With her head throbbing in pain and her body begging for rest, Sarah opened the front door and looked out into the raging snowstorm. "How am I going to get to Steve Mintfield's?" she asked herself, fearful of the deep snow and deadly winds.

Sophia reached into the pocket of her ski pants and pulled out a key. "Take my snowmobile. It's parked in your backyard."

Sarah turned and looked at Sophia. "You're not a bad woman," she told her. "But you really messed up."

"I know...and I'm willing to pay for my mistakes." Sophia tossed Sarah the snowmobile key. "Hurry, okay? Conrad may be a jerk, but...save him for me."

"I will," Sarah said. "Amanda, if I'm not back by tonight..."

"I'll call for help," Amanda promised.

Sarah gave Amanda a weak smile and stepped out into the snow, closing the front door behind her. The winds immediately began stealing her body heat. "Hold on Conrad, I'm coming."

Holding her head with her left hand, Sarah trudged out into the deep snow and made her way around to the back of her cabin where a red snowmobile sat waiting for her.

chapter nine

Conrad watched the man with dark, wavy black hair —much like his own—pace back and forth in front of the cold fireplace. "You thought you were smarter than me, didn't you?" Frank yelled at Mitch. "But I was smarter. I waited you out. I had McQuire cancel your bank card to starve you out. I broke you, boy!"

Mitch shook his head. "Being hungry didn't weaken me. I remained here because I love Sophia. I have always loved Sophia and I always will. It's because of me that McQuire tortured her. If...she would have just given me her diary, I could have ended this stupid game."

"Don't play games with me," Frank yelled. He pointed a gun at Mitch. "I want the diary. Sophia told me she gave her diary to you, so don't play with me. I tracked you to the woman cop's cabin, didn't I? I figured it was only a matter of time before you went to her, and I was right. So don't play with me, boy. I want the diary and I want it now!"

Conrad looked at the gray ski suit Frank was wearing. The guy was ready to kill and run. The living room he and Mitch were in, tied to two wooden kitchen chairs, was empty except for a sleeping bag shoved into the far right corner. It was clear that Frank was ready to clear out at a moment's notice. "Mitch told me he has Sophia's diary," Conrad said.

"You liar," Mitch growled at Conrad. "Stop lying. I told you all that I know, Frank. Sophia backed out on me. She called Gatti and informed him that you were going to try and put him in the dirt. She wanted Gatti to offer her protection against McQuire. But Gatti isn't stupid. He knows going against McQuire would be a huge mistake."

"Gatti came here searching for Sophia and you," Conrad told Frank. "I didn't realize that until last night. Gatti knew that Sophia wasn't dead all along, but he knew that he had to take her out, along with you."

"Gatti is history," Frank snapped. "I have everything worked out with McQuire. McQuire is sick of Gatti and Sarti. I'm the new man in town. Only McQuire doesn't know he's going to eat a bullet along with Gatti."

"You're insane," Mitch said. "You're going to cause a war."

"Exactly," Frank grinned, looking at Mitch with his gray, bloodshot eyes. "When my war is over, I'll have control over everyone."

"McQuire set Gatti up and fed him false data. But he had help. A certain Chief Cunningham seemed to take a quick vacation, didn't he? How much did McQuire bribe the chief?" Conrad asked. "But the chief isn't stupid...scared and weak, but not stupid. He changed the weather conditions on the death report, leaving that as a clue for me. I thought the Feds had changed the weather around on the report, but it was Chief Cunningham, trying to tell his people something was amiss."

Frank gritted his teeth. "I'll deal with that old man later."

"Not on my watch," Conrad promised.

"And what are you going to do?" Frank yelled, aiming his gun at Conrad. "I should have killed my sister when I had the chance. But I had to use her. I knew she was going to call Gatti. I needed Gatti to become suspicious of McQuire."

"Gatti will never kill McQuire," Mitch warned.

"Is that so?" Frank asked. "Gatti bought McQuire's headstone the moment he found out my sister was alive."

Conrad stared at Frank in disgust. "You killed an innocent woman. Life doesn't matter to you. You're going to pay."

"I killed a two-bit actress working local plays for pennies," Frank said, sounding pleased with himself. "I took that failed woman, tied her up to a tree, waited for her to freeze to death, and then placed her body next to a rock. And who will know? Who will care? Where are the reporters flashing her name all over the news, Spencer? Huh? I killed a woman with no family and no life. I did her a favor."

"You're going to pay," Conrad repeated. "I'm taking you all down. Gatti, McQuire, Sophia, all of you."

A sudden knock came at the front door. Frank tensed up. "Who's there?" he yelled, backing up to the fireplace.

A tall, thin man with short gray hair wearing a thick black coat walked into the cabin. "I'm here," Agent McQuire announced. "And so is Gatti."

Conrad saw that McQuire was pressing a gun against Gatti's back. "You're all dead," Gatti roared.

"Inside," McQuire ordered him.

Gatti walked further into the living room. McQuire kicked the front door shut with his right boot. "Okay, Frank, it ends here. I want the diary in exchange for Gatti."

Gatti looked at Conrad and then at Mitch and said nothing. Mitch shook his head at Gatti. "You're going down, Gatti. You're going to prison."

"Shut up," Gatti warned. "Next time I'll sink you in the river myself."

Conrad looked past Gatti at the living room window. The daylight outside was turning dark. "I have Davis and Young taking Gatti's boys back to New York," McQuire informed

Frank. "The hicks at the police station were given a Federal Order releasing Gatti into my custody. We're in the clear. Now, give me the diary and I'll look the other way and let you create your war."

Struggling against the ropes holding his wrists together, Conrad knew that he had to act, but how? "Untie me, Frank," he yelled, "and we'll wrestle man to man."

Frank shook his head at Conrad. "Shut your mouth," he said and focused back on McQuire. "Okay, McQuire, here's the diary." He pointed his gun at McQuire.

"What do you think you're doing, Frank?" McQuire asked, without any fear in his voice. "You dare betray me?"

"I'm in control now." Frank grinned and began to fire. As he did, a rock smashed through the front window.

"I have the diary!" Sarah yelled through the broken window.

"I'm awful sorry I didn't tell you I took that woman's book," Steve said from where he stood behind a tree next to Sarah. "I just didn't want those FBI guys getting to it. I could tell they were bad. I guess I talked a bit too much yesterday morning."

"It's okay," Sarah said. She nodded at the rifle Steve was holding. "You just get ready to cover me."

"Yes, ma'am," Steve promised.

Sarah turned to Andrew and Edwin and instructed them to cover the back exit of the cabin. She looked down at the brown diary in her hands. She opened it and began to read page 1 in a loud voice. "'Today I heard Gatti and Frank talking about holding up a cash shipment...'"

"Way to go, Sarah," Conrad whispered.

"She has the diary," Frank yelled at McQuire. "Sophia gave the diary to that stupid cop woman! We have to stop her!"

Sarah kept reading as Andrew and Edwin circled around to the back of the cabin with their guns at the ready. When she came to the end of page 1, she stopped and called through the window, "Frank, send Conrad out or I'll send this diary to every news agency in the country."

Frank exploded. He ran to the living room window and began firing into the snow. Gatti spun around and faced McQuire. "Shoot me or give me a gun," he growled.

McQuire shoved Gatti down onto the floor and hurried over to Conrad. Yanking a pocket knife out of his front coat pocket, he began to cut Conrad loose. "Get out there and get me that diary or you're all dead," he ordered Conrad.

"What are you doing?" Frank yelled.

McQuire pointed his gun at Frank. "Drop your gun, Frank. Now."

Conrad broke free of his ropes and stood up. McQuire nodded at the front door. "Get outside," he repeated and began to back away from Conrad. As he did, Mitch threw out both legs in front of him. McQuire tripped and stumbled backward. Gatti was on him before he even hit the floor.

Frank released the clip from his gun and went for the second clip in his coat pocket. Conrad rushed at Frank before he could reload and took him down to the floor. Frank began struggling with Conrad. "You're nothing...you're weak!" he yelled.

Conrad raised his right fist into the air and knocked Frank unconscious with one hard hit. "And you're through," he said, scrambling to his feet. As he did, Gatti stood up holding McQuire's gun.

"Who should I kill first?" Gatti asked.

"Coward!" Mitch yelled. "I almost defeated you. All I needed was Sophia's diary."

"Send Conrad out," Sarah yelled from outside. "Frank, this is my last warning."

Gatti stared at Conrad. There was a pause, and McQuire,

who had been pretending to be hurt, seized the opportunity. He eased his hand into his coat pocket and pulled out a small pistol. "Gatti," he growled and fired the pistol.

Gatti grabbed his right shoulder and dropped the gun in his hand. Conrad dived to the floor, grabbed the gun, and got off a shot at McQuire just as McQuire prepared to fire at him. McQuire dropped his pistol and grabbed his right hand with his left. "My hand," he cried out.

"Sarah, get in here!" Conrad yelled out through the living room window.

"Stay here," Sarah told Steve and hurried through the deep snow toward the front door of the cabin.

Conrad opened the front door and smiled at her. "You arrived just in time, Detective Garland."

Sarah smiled back at Conrad and hugged his neck. As she did, Andrew and Edwin came bursting in through the back door and charged into the living room. "They're all yours," Sarah told Andrew, pointing at Frank, Gatti, and McQuire. "And this," she added, turning to Mitch and holding up the diary, "is all yours." She tossed the diary into Mitch's lap. "Go write your story."

"But..." Andrew began, confused. He was tired, covered in snow, and half frozen. The last thing he needed was more questions.

"Unless we let Mitch write his story," Conrad warned, "these three thugs will come back for us in full force when they get out of prison. We have to let the press take them down."

"You're all dead," Gatti promised.

Mitch smiled proudly. "No, Gatti," he said, "you're the one that's dead. By the time I'm finished with you, there will be absolutely nothing left but a few scraps for the prison dogs to eat."

Gatti stared at Mitch, and for the first time in his life, he knew that his threats meant absolutely nothing.

"Arrest these people," McQuire ordered Andrew. "And get me to a hospital, now!"

Andrew walked over to McQuire, helped him stand up, and then slapped a pair of handcuffs on him. "You have the right to remain silent, you scumbag," he said.

Sarah drew in a deep breath. "Well," she said to Conrad, looking down at Frank, "I can't say that we won. That man lying on the floor nearly killed all of us."

Conrad glanced down at Frank. "He was always a clever person. But his temper was his enemy."

Steve stuck his head through the front door. "Mighty cold outside," he said. "The storm seems to be letting up a little, though."

Sarah looked at Steve. It amazed her that a simple cabinet builder, of all people, had taken the diary of this strange and beautiful woman. And who could have known? No one. "Thank you for being an honest man," she told Steve. "If you hadn't confessed to taking the diary, I don't know what I would have done."

Conrad looked at Steve's frozen face in shock. "*He* had Sophia's diary?"

"I'll explain later," Sarah promised, rubbing the back of her sore head. "I think I have a concussion." She walked back out into the snow. Looking up into the dark sky, she allowed the snow to fall onto her beautiful face and let the feeling of the icy snowflakes on her skin shut down her mind.

"Well, New York," Amanda said, propping her feet up on Conrad's desk, "all's well that ends well. Sophia is back in the Witness Protection Program. Mitch is writing his story. Gatti, Frank, and McQuire, along with all of their thugs, are behind bars. And we're still alive. I just hate the fact that Sophia's terrible brother had everyone chasing their tails, looking in every direction but the right one. But, I guess we came out okay."

Conrad tossed down the pencil he was holding. "Frank was forcing everyone to become enemies while remaining invisible. He knows how to play the game. What he didn't count on was Sophia turning against him in the end. I guess that woman does have a conscience...somewhere inside of her heart."

"Thank goodness Sophia started her diary. And thank goodness Mr. Stick Hands decided to give Sophia's diary to Los Angeles."

"Mr. Mintfield meant well," Conrad assured Amanda. "He's a good man."

Standing at the office window wearing a warm blue sweater and looking out into the snow, Sarah thought about Frank. "Conrad, are you going back to New York, now that Frank is being sent to prison?"

Conrad picked up his brown coffee mug and took a sip. "No," he answered. "The truth is, I've kinda become fond of this little town. I'm not anxious to go back to pulling bodies out of dirty alleys."

Sarah smiled. As she admired the softly falling snow outside, she felt a warm spot appear in her heart. Life sure was different in Alaska, she thought. She spotted a group of teenagers throwing snowballs at each other as they ran down the street toward the diner. "Good," she told Conrad. "I'm glad."

Amanda winked at Conrad but didn't say a word. Conrad smiled and put down his coffee just as Andrew popped his head into the office. His face was urgent and serious. "Park Ranger was found dead out near Clear Diamond Lake."

Sarah turned away from the window and looked at Conrad. Conrad nodded his head and stood up. "Come on, ladies," he said. "We've got another case."

Amanda slumped down in her chair. "Jack, hurry up and get home," she groaned.

Sarah walked to Amanda and patted her best friend on the shoulder. "Come on, June Bug, we're a team."

Amanda glanced up at Sarah's face and then looked at Conrad. Conrad tipped her a wink. "Fine, sure, I'm coming." She stood up. "But one of these days I'm going on holiday far away from the both of you."

Without saying another word, Amanda walked out of the office. Sarah and Conrad made eye contact and then followed Amanda out into the hallway. As they did, their hands touched slightly. Sarah didn't mind, and neither did Conrad.

Far away, riding down a snowy trail on a snowmobile, a man wearing a black ski suit began whistling to himself.

more from wendy

Alaska Cozy Mystery Series

Maple Hills Cozy Series

Sweeetfern Harbor Cozy Series

Sweet Peach Cozy Series

Sweet Shop Cozy Series

Twin Berry Bakery Series

about wendy meadows

Wendy Meadows is a USA Today bestselling author whose stories showcase women sleuths. To date, she has published dozens of books, which include her popular Sweetfern Harbor series, Sweet Peach Bakery series, and Alaska Cozy series, to name a few. She lives in the "Granite State" with her husband, two sons, two mini pigs and a lovable Labradoodle.

Join Wendy's newsletter to stay up-to-date with new releases. As a subscriber, you'll also get BLACKVINE MANOR, the complete series, for FREE!

Join Wendy's Newsletter Here
wendymeadows.com/cozy

Made in the USA
Monee, IL
26 January 2023

26332379R00056